BIRTHDAY BOOK CLUB

Donated by:

KRISTIN KAREE

November 7, 1988

D1511070

STREETS *of* GOLD

by Karen Branson

G.P. PUTNAM'S SONS • NEW YORK

Library of Congress Cataloging in Publication Data
Branson, Karen.
Streets of gold.
Summary: Fourteen-year-old Maureen and her family,
refugees from the Irish potato famine of the 1840's,
arrive in New York and struggle to make a place for
themselves in an environment more hostile than they had
imagined.
[1. Emigration and immigration–Fiction. 2. Irish
Americans–Fiction. 3. New York (N.Y.)–Fiction]
I. Title.
PZ7.B73756St 1981 [Fic] 81-13963
ISBN 0-399-20791-0 AACR2
First Impression

Contents

For Kathleen and Jennifer,
and also for Barry

1
On Board the Western Star

Maureen O'Connor opened her eyes. The hold was dark and for a moment she could not remember where she was. Then the ship rose on a swell and her stomach churned uneasily. "Aye," she groaned, "the *Western Star.*"

Dirty straw covered the bunk Maureen shared with her brother Paddy. The straw poked through the blanket, prickling her arms and legs. Maureen wrinkled her nose. Even after all these weeks at sea, the straw smelled of cattle.

Not to wonder: Captain Baggett had put the immigrants in the same quarters formerly occupied by livestock, never bothering to clean out the hold first. The only difference now was that his human cargo had a place to sleep: narrow bunks crammed one atop the other with but a few inches breathing space between them.

Da and Brian slept in the bunk directly over Maureen and Paddy. The wooden slats creaked as Da shifted his weight. Da's long legs are burden enough for that small bed, thought Maureen. Just as well Brian is a slight lad and takes little room.

Maureen felt Paddy's knees against her back and rolled over, trying to find a more comfortable position. It was no use. Paddy, like Da, was large-boned and crowded the bunk's small space. Maureen drew herself into a tight ball and tugged at the blanket which Paddy had wrapped around himself.

Something had awakened her and she realized now that it was the sound of the storm. She listened to the screeching wind as it battered the *Star*, forcing the ship to labor in the heavy seas. "*Och*, that wind puts me in mind of a *banshee*," she whispered. She could hear the thud of footsteps up on deck as the sailors ran to and fro.

The *Star* was taking on water. Maureen listened to it slapping against the bilge as the ship listed one way and then the other. She shuddered. What if the water forced the rats farther into the hold where the passengers slept? She had heard them scrambling back and forth and more than once had seen their tiny eyes glinting from the shadows.

"Oh, Ma," Maureen cried softly, muffling her voice with the blanket. "I wish we'd stayed in Ireland with you. Sure this old ship is doomed."

In the weeks since sailing from Cork City, Maureen had often regretted leaving Ireland and her mother behind. She could picture Ma standing before the hearth, her face rosy from the glowing coals. There would be porridge on the table and newly dug praties bubbling over the fire. Maureen closed her eyes, wanting to hold fast to this memory. But the grim truth of how things had really been intruded: every potato black with rot; Da's oats and wheat given to the English landlord; the harsh winter with nothing to eat. Worst of all was the sickness that accompanied the famine, sniffing out weakened bodies like a wolf stalking an easy prey.

Little sister Rosheen had died in the spring. After that,

Ma had grown weaker, and one day she had spoken to Da about what must be done. "Sean, take Maureen and the boys to America, before it is too late," she had said. "I will follow when I am able, God willing."

Suddenly the *Star* pitched forward and Maureen gripped the sides of the bunk, fearing this time the ship would overturn entirely. She held her breath and waited. From a neighboring berth came the sound of Timmy Kelly heaving his guts into a bucket.

Maureen heard Mrs. Kelly crooning to her son, telling him he'd be well by morning. Maureen shook her head sadly. Timmy had been sick for many days and everyone in the hold knew that he was dying.

The soft cadence of the rosary came from the Kelly's direction. "Aye, his ma knows, too," Maureen whispered. "St. Brigid help her."

Paddy twisted in his sleep, pulling the blanket. Maureen held onto it and gave the boy a poke. "Paddy, mind the blanket, will you?" she muttered crossly.

He babbled a few words and quieted, but was soon tossing and turning again. Maureen frowned. It wasn't like Paddy to be so restless.

Morning came and the storm continued to hound the ship. The rain drummed noisily on the deck overheard while the oil lamps cast their gloomy light into the hold. Maureen sighed. How she dreaded another long day spent in the smelly confines. "At least when I go topside for our rations I can have a breath of air," she told herself, "even if it means getting wet, as well."

Da swung himself down from the upper bunk and landed on the floor alongside Maureen. He rubbed his neck. "Och, daughter," he said, "last night was the devil's own. 'Tis a wonder we're still afloat, what with the water coming in everywhere."

"Aye, Da," Maureen answered, climbing over Paddy to

9

get out of the bunk. Her legs were stiff and she moved them awkwardly. " 'Tis like an old woman I am," she complained. Her woolen skirt hung loosely about her hips; the months of hunger also showed in her pale, hollow cheeks. Yet there was still something pretty about her: a softness in her green eyes and a bonny lilt in the arch of her brow.

Maureen glanced down at Paddy. "You lazy thing," she teased. "Time to wake up." Nudging him, her hand felt very warm. She laid it against the boy's cheek, then withdrew it quickly. "Da, he's on fire!"

Sean O'Connor bent over his son. "Paddy? What is it, lad?"

The boy opened his eyes. "Dada, my throat hurts," he croaked. "And I'm so thirsty."

Da looked anxiously at Maureen. She took Paddy's hand and her brother slowly turned his head, his eyes following the trickles of water that ran down the sides of the hold. Maureen thought of Timmy Kelly and a chilling fear seeped into her heart.

Brian was awake now and leaning over the edge of the bunk. "That one still asleep?" he asked, pointing at Paddy.

"Aye," answered Maureen. "I fear he's not well."

"Huh. He was himself yesterday when we played chase-the-pig. Paddy won every time." Brian slid down from the bunk and pulled on his trousers before going off to the toilet buckets.

Maureen watched Brian make his way among the passengers. Short and dark-haired, he was twelve years old, nearly two years older than Paddy. Yet Brian was the smaller of the boys. Paddy was tall and sturdily built, like Da, and strode about with the same robust manner. He even had Da's thatch of sandy hair and lively blue eyes. But as Maureen looked at the limp body lying on the bunk now, she saw only a wan, dispirited likeness of her brother.

Da stroked the boy's forehead, brushing back the matted hair. "There, son," he murmured, "sure you'll be all right, eh? A big boy-o like yourself?"

Maureen heard a sailor opening the hatch. She reached for the kettle. "Da, I'd best go for the rations now," she said, wrapping her shawl around her shoulders and running toward the ladder.

Coming onto the deck, Maureen was pelted by the steady rain. The wind caught her long black hair, whipping it about her face so she could barely see. She struggled across to the women queued near the water barrel. Her shawl afforded scant protection from the rain and she prayed the line would move quickly.

The sailor tending the rations was dressed in a long oiled slicker that shed the rain to either side. His solemn eyes peered out at Maureen from under the brimmed cap. She recognized him as the young sailor who'd clambered high up the rigging her first day at sea. She had watched him that morning with astonishment, for he'd gone hand over hand as if hopping a mere hedgerow.

He was a tall, handsome lad, with fine white teeth and a faraway sort of look to him. Maureen had been struck by how young he seemed. He appeared to be little older than herself and she was but fourteen. One day she had commented to Da, "Yon sailor there? Sure he's very young to be at sea, with only the other sailors for a family?"

Now she brushed the rain from her eyes and held her kettle out to the sailor. He ladled water into it and turned to the case of hardtack bread. As he opened the lid he looked up at Maureen.

"Have you a means of keeping the 'tack dry, miss?" he asked.

The rain had completely drenched Maureen's shawl.

11

Her hair clung to her shoulders and bits of straw from the hold were caught in it. She looked down at her damp, rumpled skirt. "No matter," she murmured, "for all else is wet."

The sailor paused, then put his hand inside his slicker. "Wait," he said, pulling out a navy kerchief. Quickly wrapping her hardtack in the kerchief, he smiled and gave it to Maureen. "Here. Perhaps this will help."

Maureen felt her cheeks reddening. "Why, 'tis kind of you, indeed." She tucked the hardtack under her arm. Looking at the sailor, she noticed that his eyes were gray, very like the color of the storm-tossed sea. "Many thanks," she added. Maureen turned and moved cautiously toward the hatch, fearing she might lose her footing on the slippery deck. She hesitated at the ladder, glancing shyly back at the sailor before descending into the hold.

2
A Watery Grave

The Widow Fitzpatrick was standing over Paddy when Maureen returned. Maureen drew in her breath. Wearing a long black dress, her mane of gray hair loose about her shoulders, the Widow looked frightfully like a *banshee.* In Gaelic, *banshee* meant "fairy woman," and Maureen knew from Ma's stories that the *banshee's* cry foretold the coming of death.

The Widow Fitzpatrick was no *banshee,* but she was peculiar. She muttered strange words and spent many hours sitting by herself, moving five small stones around a piece of black cloth. Da said the smooth white stones were used for laying curses. "Aye, and in the old days a widow's curse was more feared than any other," he had added. Hearing this, Maureen was reluctant to get too close to the Widow Fitzpatrick.

But the old woman was wise in the ways of sickness and had brought an assortment of healing herbs with her on the *Star.* She studied Paddy shrewdly. "Your tongue, lad, let me see it," she ordered. The boy winced and stuck out his tongue. "Humph," the Widow said, frowning. "Well, no need to leave it there all morning. Back in."

13

She hunched over Paddy and pressed her hands against his face and neck. After a minute she straightened and turned to Da. "I can't say certain what ails him, though 'tis likely rotten throat. I'll give him dried bitters, but what he needs is lemon juice to cut that choking phlegm. Aye, and a salt sock to lay on his neck."

Da nodded grimly. Maureen remembered that Ma had once traded her best *bauneen* yarn for a basket of lemons, saying lemon drink was a cure better than any other. She eyed the disheveled passengers sitting amongst their belongings. Of course no one had any lemons, not here in the middle of the ocean! Nor could Maureen hope to find a sock filled with hot salt to wrap around Paddy's neck.

She chewed on her lip. There was nothing to give Paddy except the foul-smelling water and hardtack. "An unlikely cure, I'm thinking."

Paddy spent a restless day. Maureen tried to cool his forehead with a damp cloth but the fever kept a fierce grip on him.

That evening Maureen was aware of a strange stillness in the Kelly family's berth. Then she noticed Mrs. Kelly weeping and clutching her rosary beads. Mr. Kelly sat next to her, his face a wash of sorrow. Maureen looked at Timmy Kelly's stiffened body and knew what had happened.

"Faded away, he did," was all Mrs. Kelly could say when Maureen and Da went over to comfort the family.

Maureen dreaded what was to come. It was sad enough with no priest to give the boy's soul a decent parting, but to throw him to a watery grave seemed cruel indeed.

"Would you want help?" Da said gently to the boy's mother.

Mrs. Kelly nodded and got out a brush for Timmy's

matted hair. Maureen started buttoning his shirt. Two buttons were missing and she looked questioningly at Da. Was there time to replace them?

Da nodded and she quickly went over to her sack, drawing out her sewing box. In a few minutes the shirt was mended. Maureen neatly tucked it in and straightened the collar. She was glad Da was there to help her, for she found minding the dead a difficult task and wished the ordeal was over. "Ah, little one," she said to the boy's shrunken body, "I meant nothing against you."

Word came that it was time to go on deck for the burial. Mrs. Kelly smoothed out the blanket while Da lifted Timmy onto it. Mr. Kelly helped wrap the boy, but could not bring himself to cover his face. "We'll come up with you," Da said.

It was nearly dark. The wind no longer blew with gale force, but the rain fell steadily on the darkened deck.

Neither Captain Baggett nor his first mate, Mr. Hawkins, were to be seen. Maureen was glad for that. Too often she had heard Mate Hawkins taunting the passengers or gibing at the sailors in a cruel way. He's no man to offer a kind word, thought Maureen.

An old, toothless sailor dressed in oilskins beckoned the Kellys forward. He cleared his throat. "I'm sorry for your trouble," he said, leaning over so Mrs. Kelly could hear him.

The comment surprised Maureen, for it was an Irish expression, said when a loved one has died.

The sailor waited while the families prayed. Mr. Kelly held his son and Mrs. Kelly stood next to him, stroking the boy's wet blanket. Then Da took Timmy from Mr. Kelly's arms and gently lifted him to the bulwarks.

Maureen was thankful that darkness had settled over the deck. She did not want to see the moment when

15

Timmy hung in midair just before dropping. There was silence, and then a dull splash as his body hit the water. Maureen closed her eyes and murmured a prayer for Timmy's soul.

Maureen could not sleep that night. Although she knew it was her mind playing tricks, she kept hearing a child's small voice crying from somewhere outside the ship. She pulled the blanket over her head and covered her ears. The crying persisted and Maureen reached under the bunk, groping for her satchel. In it was the wooden crucifix Ma had given her. "Take this to America," Ma had said, "it will be a comfort to you in the new cottage."

Maureen found the crucifix and held it to her breast. "God keep Rosheen and Timmy in Heaven, God be with Mammy, God protect our Paddy and make him well. . . ."

3
Lemons From a Sailor

For three days and nights the storm continued to torment the faltering ship. Paddy's eyes grew dim and Maureen feared for him. She remembered what the Widow Fitzpatrick had said about lemon juice being an aid for rotten throat. Could there be lemons in the *Star*'s pantry? And if so, was there any way she could get some for Paddy? The question vexed Maureen. Last week Mate Hawkins had ordered a man flogged for stealing a small piece of jerky from the pantry. Dare she risk a similar fate?

Toward sunset Maureen slipped open the hatch cover and crept up on deck. The sea was less stormy now, but the skies continued to pour great buckets of rain onto the ship. At least the wet gray curtain kept Maureen from being easily seen and she was grateful for that.

Her head down, she scrambled over the rigging that lay coiled on the deck. The rough wet ropes scraped her hands. Nearby, a voice called out and Maureen froze. The call came again, this time answered by another sailor. She waited a moment, then edged up toward the captain's galley.

She listened. All was quiet. She took a deep breath and

dashed up the galley steps. Just as she reached the top, Maureen found herself looking into a sailor's astonished eyes.

She blinked. It was the young sailor who had given her his kerchief to protect the hardtack a few days before.

For an instant neither Maureen nor the sailor moved. Then he grabbed her and pulled her inside the galley.

"Are you daft, girl? You're not supposed to be here. You'd better get below before the mate sees you."

"Please, listen to me," Maureen pleaded. "My brother is terribly sick. I'm only asking for a few lemons to help him get well."

The sailor stared at her. "You're what? No, I'm sorry; I can't give you anything. The mate has strict orders—"

Maureen pulled her arm away. "Oh, bother the mate; he doesn't care what happens to us. But I'll not let him take our Paddy!" She ran into the larder before the sailor could stop her.

He came after Maureen and spun her around. "You *are* daft. Hawkins will have you flogged if he finds you here."

Maureen's eyes searched the pantry shelves. Suddenly she saw exactly what she wanted. A small net bag filled with lemons hung from a wall peg. "Mister, please, a few lemons won't be missed."

"You don't know Mr. Hawkins. He'd miss the shine off an apple. Wily he is, too; he'll find you out."

"I don't care! Do you think I want my own brother thrown into that cold ocean?"

The sailor kept a tight grip on Maureen's arm. Maureen saw the line of his jaw harden. He muttered something, then jerked his head toward the bag of lemons.

"Blasted immigrant ships," he said, letting go of her arm. He reached up, took four lemons from the bag, and thrust them at her.

His action startled Maureen. She hesitated a moment before speaking. "I . . . I thank you," she said, taking the lemons and backing away. "A hundred blessings on you, sir, and on all your kin."

In the light of the oil lamp Maureen saw the sailor glance warily at the door. "Please, go," he whispered, "before Mate Hawkins catches you."

Maureen turned and ran down onto the main deck. She stumbled across to the hatchway, her heart pounding. She did not see the dark silhouette watching her from the quarterdeck landing.

4
Memories of Ireland

Maureen was glad that the light from the sooty oil lamps was feeble. She was able to creep down the hatchway steps and move across to the O'Connors' berth without anyone taking notice of her.

She knelt down next to Paddy. Da, grim-faced, sat close by.

"Dada," Maureen whispered, "see what I have." Turning toward Paddy, she reached into her damp bodice and pulled out the four lemons then quickly put them beneath the blanket out of view.

"Jesus, Mary and Joseph," Da breathed. "You didn't steal—"

"No, no. A sailor gave them to me. I told him about Paddy."

Da looked cautiously over his shoulder. "*Gave* them to you? Does the mate know?"

Maureen paused. "I . . . I think not. Da, 'tis only four lemons. Sure there was a bag full of them."

Da lowered his voice. "Mind you keep them well hidden, daughter. Not a word of this to anyone or there could be trouble."

Maureen frowned. "Aye, Da."

Maureen halved the lemons with Da's knife. Keeping her back to the other passengers, she squeezed the juice into a cup. All at once the lemons' tangy fragrance pierced the hold's stale air.

Two neighboring women glanced up, their noses twitching. Da slowly stood and positioned himself in such a way as to block Maureen from their view.

Paddy opened his eyes and Maureen bent close to him. "Paddy, I've lemon juice for you."

A small hoarse sound came from the boy.

Maureen mixed a little water with the juice and held the cup to Paddy's lips. He winced as he attempted to swallow. Maureen urged him on and finally the cup was empty.

"Ah, good boy," she said. "I'll give you more tomorrow."

Kevin Mahoney came over to the O'Connors' berth. He was from Mallow and had met Da while waiting to board the *Star* in Cork City. Kevin had a gruff manner but Maureen had also seen a melancholy look in his heavy-lidded eyes. The poor man had lost his wife and only child to the famine.

"Your Brian is across the way," Kevin said, "entertaining the young 'uns. That boy tells 'The Kildare Pooka' better than anyone I've heard."

"Oh, aye," said Da, "he's a magic way with words, the same as his mother." Da shook his head sadly. "Ah, Mary *machree*," he murmured, "may the saints protect you."

Maureen looked up at her father. She could tell from his voice that he was troubled about having left Ma in Ireland. But at least there was comfort in knowing that Ma was with her brother Owen and his family. Better than being on this smelly old ship.

"Sean, how is the lad?" asked Kevin.

Da shifted uneasily. Tall and roughly hewn, he was a man used to being out-of-doors: cutting turf, tilling the rocky soil, thatching a worn roof. For him, the dark hold was a prison. "He's about the same, I'm thinking."

Kevin nodded in sympathy. "Aye. The poor lad."

Da patted his son's arm. "Once we reach America, all will be well, eh Paddy?"

"Pray God that's so," Maureen whispered.

Kevin's face, like Da's, was covered with a "sea-crossing beard." He rubbed his hand across the stubbly growth. "Sean, I've been thinking," he said, "of how it was in Ireland before the praties failed us. A man could be happy then."

"Oh, aye," Da agreed with a bitter laugh. "If the landlord didn't put him on the road. Twelve years I gave working that land, making the cottage a decent home so some fat English lord could buy another horse for riding to hounds!"

Da's voice grew weary. "A man doesn't forget such things, Kevin. There we were, the praties rotted, winter coming on. Still, I had to send my oat crop to England for the rent, and watch my family starve."

Maureen had often heard this story, and others like it. They were all the same: raise grain to pay the English landlord, grow praties to feed the family. A potato bed took little tending; it was "the farmer's friend" and gave a bountiful yield. Then the awful blight struck and the fields turned black.

Back home, when Da condemned the English, Ma scolded him. Her brother had lived in England, so she knew a bit about life there. She said little English boys were sold to mastersweeps and made to climb inside clogged chimneys. If a lad resisted, a straw fire would be set under him. And what of the girls in the cotton mills, tied to their looms from dawn to dusk? Sure they didn't come to Ireland for country sport, Ma would say.

Ma's words could make you think differently about things. Even now, Maureen had to admit that she didn't wish harm to the young sailor who'd given her the lemons, even though he was as English as Mate Hawkins.

Over near the hatchway steps a crowd of passengers had gathered. In the dim lamplight Maureen caught a glimpse of burnished wood. One of the men was taking out his fiddle.

" 'Tis Conor the Fiddler!" a boy shouted.

Faces turned toward the steps. All at once Conor's fiddle let go a reel and the music filled the hold.

Da nudged Maureen's arm. "Go give a listen, daughter. I'll sit with Paddy. Go on."

The music was hard to resist. Maureen smiled at Da. "I will, then."

She hurried over to join the passengers surrounding the musician. His tune was one she recognized from the fair day in Mallow. "How lively 'tis, even down here," she said to the woman beside her.

The woman wiped her eyes. "Oh, aye. It puts me in mind of my first dress from the manty-maker," she said. "God love us, weren't those courting days?"

Maureen nodded. It was good to recall the happy times, to remember Ireland as it had once been.

The fiddler paused to wipe his brow and one of the men shouted to him, "Hey, Conor, how about a rebel song?"

There was a chorus of approval and shouts of "Free Ireland!" came from every corner. Conor grinned, then put resin on his bow and lifted the fiddle to his chin. The notes came softly at first, but soon swelled into a rousing call to battle.

"Death to every foe and traitor . . ." sang the men, stamping their feet. "*Arrah,* me boys, for freedom, 'tis the rising of the moon!"

Maureen's cheeks flushed. She looked around the hold, at the faces of the men and women, and all at once her eyes filled with tears. She turned away from the fiddle player and the music. "Such a place for rebel songs," she murmured, "here, on a ship going to America. Sure we'll none of us see Ireland again."

5
Out of the Hold

The next day Maureen gave Paddy more of the lemon juice mixed with water. "Good lad," she said, holding the cup to his lips. "If ever this storm ends and we've the cookstoves again, I'll fix you a bit of porridge as well, eh?"

Paddy gave a weak grunt. "My throat still hurts."

"I know, pet. But sure the lemons will soon help."

Maureen jumped when a voice sounded close behind her. The Widow Fitzpatrick was there, carefully eyeing Paddy. "Ah, better, is he?" she said with a sly look at the lemon drink.

Maureen wondered if she should explain the lemons to the Widow. She watched uncertainly as the Widow's bony fingers felt Paddy's forehead.

"Aye, 'tis rotten throat he has, the same as the rest of them," the Widow said, waving her hand to include the other sick passengers. "But this lad's too crafty for such to take him."

The rounded hump of her shoulders forced the Widow's head forward. Her face was so close that Maureen could see herself reflected in the woman's eyes.

"He's going to be all right," the Widow whispered,

smiling as if in possession of a secret. "I know about such things." Then without another word, the old woman took her stick and hobbled back to her corner.

Brian came and sat beside Maureen. "Begone!" he said, swatting at his head where a flea was annoying him.

Maureen looked at the flea bites on her arm. "Oh, Brian, what will we do at all?" she cried. "I can't bear another day in this wretched hold."

Brian shrugged. "The storm can't last forever." He looked over at his brother. "*Arrah*, Paddy? Would you be wanting a story? I could tell 'The Brewery of Eggshells' if you like. 'Tis one Ma got from Grandfar, remember?"

Paddy's eyelids fluttered and he slowly nodded his head.

"Well enough, then." Brian scratched at his flea bites and moved next to Paddy. "Now, 'twas once a cunning woman by the name of Gray Ellen . . ."

Maureen could not help but smile, thinking how much Brian resembled Ma just now. Aye, it would please her to know that Grandfar's tales were also making the journey to America.

A trio of young girls came tiptoeing to within earshot of Brian and Paddy. "Psst, Brian, can we give a listen?" the oldest girl inquired. "Sure we'll not be any bother."

Brian indicated a spot well away from Paddy. "Aye, sit there. But mind you stay clear of this fellow, for he's part dragon and might breathe his old fire on you."

The children shrunk back and settled themselves, all the while keeping a cautious eye on Paddy.

While listening to Brian's story Maureen noticed a peculiar silence in the hold. She stood and looked around. Other passengers were doing the same; talking had ceased and the immigrants stared at one another with hopeful faces. Maureen listened. The rain hammering against the deck—had it finally ended?

26

A wrenching noise came from the hatch as a sailor pulled the cover aside. For a moment none of the passengers moved. Then fresh air poured into the hold like a gift from Heaven, and more the miracle, blue sky could be seen through the hatch opening.

"Oh, Brian, look!" Maureen called. "At last we can be free of this place. And we'll have the stoves again!" She quickly gathered up the cookware.

Men and women crowded around the ladder, pushing their way up to the deck. Teakettles clattered against cooking pots as the passengers jostled each other. Maureen squeezed into the throng and slowly edged her way onto the ladder.

She reached the deck and stood back to get her bearings. The white sails were spread wide across the sky and a bank of gray clouds was falling back in retreat. Maureen smiled, filling her lungs with the clean salt air. "Ah!" she sighed, stretching her arms. Although the *Star* was battered from the storm, the ship began to cut a graceful westward course through the water.

The cookstoves were set up on the far side of the maindeck. Maureen went to get her ration of oats and felt a twinge of disappointment as she spotted the sailor in charge of the barrels. He was a stout fellow with a florid face and whiskers. She was hoping to see the young sailor again, the one who had given her the lemons.

The oats were infested with weevils and as Maureen cooked the porridge she attempted to pick out the tiny insects. "Pray God we'll have decent food in New York," she muttered.

Suddenly a harsh shout went up from the forecastle. It was followed by a short cracking sound, like a stick breaking. The sound came again.

Maureen frowned. Six more times she heard the sharp

crack, then silence. Not a word from the passengers or from the sailors who had stopped their work to listen.

Maureen tapped the arm of a nearby woman. "What was that, do you know?"

The woman seemed puzzled. "I'm not certain. There was a ruckus of sorts with one of the sailors. And I saw that devil Hawkins in the middle of it."

Maureen turned. Da and some other men were coming back across the deck. Da was angry, she could see that in the mottled red of his face. Mixed in with the anger was something else: a pain that deepened the lines in his brow.

Maureen went toward him. "Da, whatever was happening over there?"

Da looked away, but not before Maureen saw the sorrow in his eyes. "Yon sailor . . . he, he got in trouble. The mate saw fit to have him flogged." Da put his hand on Maureen's shoulder and pushed her toward the hatchway. "Quickly, go below, Maureen. See to your brother's porridge. This matter . . . 'tis no concern of yours."

6
Near Journey's End

A few days later as Maureen was bending over the cookstove making tea, she was aware of someone watching her. Raising her head, she saw Mate Hawkins leaning against the quarterdeck railing, his weasel eyes staring down at her. The very look of him gave her a fright. Then she thought of the lemons—what if the mate had found out about them? Maureen moved cautiously across the deck, carrying the pot of tea. Her skin prickled as she waited for the chilling sound of the mate's voice.

Maureen was not called back, nor did Mate Hawkins send one of his sailors after her. "Perhaps 'tis a foolish worry," she told herself, "to think that the man would punish me over something so small as four lemons." Still, it was a moment before she could calm herself.

Da and the boys were settled on the deck, awaiting their tea. Paddy's condition had steadily improved and each day he begged to be taken topside. Now he squirmed out from under his blanket as soon as Da's head was turned. The bright sunlight hurt his eyes but did not prevent him from making grotesque faces at the other children. All at once he yelled "Land ho!" in the manner of a sailor and laughed as the startled passengers hurried to the bulwarks.

"Hush, Paddy," Maureen hissed. "You've no call to be playing such tricks." Yet her annoyance quickly passed, for such a prank was a sign that Paddy was himself again. "Aye, and mischief is sure to follow," she added under her breath.

Kevin Mahoney approached Da and held out a portion of a letter. "Sean, here's the address of the lodging house I spoke of," he said. " 'Tis a short distance from the docks. Mrs. Duffy is a decent Irish woman; she'll not be cheating you."

"Good enough, Kevin, and thanks. Myself, I'll sleep under a hedgerow if need be. But children need a roof over them."

"Aye. If I didn't have a brother in New York, I'd be going to Mrs. Duffy's myself."

"Does the man have a job for you as well?" Da asked.

"He couldn't be certain. There's less work now on account of those like ourselves arriving each day. Many are going elsewhere to find a job."

Da nodded. "Conor told me there's hiring on the canals and in the mines. Aye, and with no English lord to take a man's shillings as fast as he earns them."

Maureen listened to Da and Kevin as she drank her tea. Would Da find a cottage like the one outside Ballyvourney, she wondered. She gazed at the steam rising from her cup. Perhaps there would be a bakery in New York that had need of a shopgirl. She could see herself wearing a fine white apron, tending to warm scones and wheaten farls; the baker telling her: "Maureen, take that currant bread home to your Da and brothers; sure I don't mind."

Maureen's mouth began to water. "*Och*, go away," she murmured, banishing the vision of a crusty scone dripping with sweet butter. She slumped down next to Brian.

"Boy-o," she said forlornly, "would you be wanting more tea?"

"Maureen?" Da called to her and pointed at a sailor up the mizzenmast. "Yon sailor, is he the one who gave you the lemons?"

She stood up and immediately recognized the lean body and the brown hair that curled from under the snug-fitting cap. "Aye, Da, 'tis the same. I . . . I don't know what name he goes by."

"He looks to be a good decent lad."

Maureen colored slightly. "Aye. I'm thinking so as well."

"He has a hard life, working under such as Hawkins," Da's voice was somber.

Maureen turned to her father. He was in low spirits today and she wondered if he'd been worrying about Ma. After the long weeks on the *Star*, Ireland seemed so far away.

She looked up at the sailor again. He was coming down the ratlines, slowly lowering himself to the deck. As he landed Maureen noticed that the lightness was gone from his step and that he moved rather stiffly. She could not help but feel a little sad, knowing she'd never see him again once she reached America.

She sighed. "Da? What sort of place is New York, do you know?"

Da wiped the salt spray from his eyes. "I can't say certain, *alanna*, but I've heard 'tis very different from Ballyvourney."

Maureen gazed out at the water. " 'Tis a wide ocean between Ireland and America." Then she noticed something floating off to the side of the ship. She squinted. It was a small wooden crate. As it came closer she could see lettering across its top.

"Da, look! What does it say?"

"New . . . York! New York!" he shouted.

His shouts brought other passengers and soon the side of the ship was lined with eager faces. A sea gull suddenly appeared, landed on the crate, and turned an inquisitive eye on the gaping crowd. The cry "New York!" went up again and the startled bird flew away. Kevin Mahoney tossed his cap into the air and whistled when the wind carried it over the bulwarks. "Sure it will reach New York before I do," he grinned.

"Da, there's a different smell in the air," Maureen declared. "Could it be because land is so near?"

Da nodded. "Aye, perhaps so." Then he let go a laugh and Maureen realized how long it had been since she'd heard a joyful sound from her father. He put his arms around her. "We're going to make it, daughter," he said, "all of us!"

7
Liam Carney Says Hello

Early the next morning the bulwarks were crowded with men, women and children watching for the first sighting of New York. All eyes strained westward as the sun climbed to twelve o'clock.

"What a sorry lot we are," thought Maureen as she looked around. There wasn't a clean face in the lot, nor one that was altogether healthy. Six weeks at sea had been difficult for even the most hardy.

Her clothes were stiff with grime and she dreamed of a tub of hot water with lots of soap. How wonderful it would be to scrub away the smell of the hold!

Paddy nudged her. "See there, Maureen?" He pointed out over the water. There was shouting and pointing from the other passengers as well.

The tip of New York's harbor was coming into view. A line of trees in green summer dress extended out along the edge of the island. Opposite them were low wharf buildings much like the structures in Cork City. Beyond the wharf stood row upon row of taller buildings, some reaching high over the tree tops, crowding the skyline.

As the *Star* edged into the harbor a hush fell over the ship. The long journey was finally ended. In one corner of the hold a child's shoe reminded Maureen of the immigrants who'd been given to the ocean's dark reaches. There was sorrow mingled with her excitement as she bid good-by and good luck to the other passengers.

Maureen reached into her pocket. In it was the kerchief the young sailor had given her to protect her hardtack during the storm. She had come upon the kerchief when tying her family's belongings together and had been uncertain how to return it.

Her eyes scanned the rigging. The sailor was not on the ropes nor did she see a sign of him elsewhere. Sadness touched her heart: he had twice shown her a great kindness and she would never even know the sailor's name.

The *Star* rocked gently beside the quay. The gangplank was let down and the passengers stepped hesitantly forward, arms filled with satchels, cookware, blankets. Maureen held her breath as her feet touched the rough-hewn wood of the dock. She took a few steps, feeling the solid ground beneath her. Turning around, she saw Brian, his eyes bright with tears. "Aye," she said, reaching her hand out to him. " 'Tis America, Brian. Truly."

Disorder greeted the immigrants as they came off the ship. An official began shouting at them to line up in front of the Immigration Entry building, a bare, confining structure with narrow windows. People jostled one another, struggling with their belongings, attempting to keep family members together. There were wails from small children and more angry shouts from the immigration officer.

Da, Maureen and the boys finally made their way into the Entry building. The hall was crowded and noisy; people stood in long lines or sat on their parcels, waiting for directions.

Not far away another shipload of immigrants was queuing up. Maureen stepped back to get a better look at them. They were fair in coloring, with the weathered skin common to country people. The women wore wide-brimmed dark bonnets. The men had long beards and black hats with flat crowns. The people were not Irish, of that Maureen was certain. Yet there was something kindred about them. She wondered if perhaps their lives had been much like her own.

The *Star* passengers were being divided into six lines and taken to the tables of medical examiners. Maureen stood on tiptoe, watching what was happening.

A man in a soiled white coat scowled at the Widow Fitzpatrick, waiting for her to unbutton her bodice. He then put a narrow black tube against her chest, with his ear next to the other end of the tube.

Da, Brian and Paddy were in the line across from Maureen. She saw Da go before the examiner. He opened his mouth, nervously watching the ceiling while the man bent over him. He was poked and looked at, then told to pass to the other side. Da jumped up with an expression of great relief.

Brian was next. A hatchet-faced attendant came alongside the doctor. She was holding a perforated tin and eyed Brian impatiently. At a nod from the doctor, she raised the tin and showered the boy with white powder, taking special care to work it into his hair.

"Nits make lice," she clucked disapprovingly.

"Next!" the woman called out, pointing her finger at Paddy.

Paddy took one small step forward. The woman reached out and yanked him by the collar, pulling him over to the doctor. A look at eyes and throat, a listen at the chest, and he was ready for dusting. He glared at the attendant as she covered him with the powder. Finally he broke away and shook himself like a wet dog.

Maureen jumped when a nearby woman let out a loud wail. The woman was clinging to her husband as the doctor chalked the letter "C" on the man's shirt.

"I'm very sorry, madam," Maureen heard the doctor say, "but those with consumption *must* be quarantined. He will get properly treated."

The man was taken to a screened area and locked inside with others who also had letters on their clothing. His wife stood by the fence, weeping.

Maureen's heart pounded as she was called before the examiner. Obediently she stepped forward and opened her mouth. The doctor leaned over. "Hmm?" he said, his breath smelling of tobacco.

Then he looked down at her bodice and gave a small nod. Maureen reddened as she undid the top buttons of her dress. He lay the black tube against her, listened, then did the same on the other side.

"Pass," he said curtly.

That was all? Thanks be to St. Brigid! Maureen quickly buttoned her dress and moved across to where Da and the boys waited. Her heart felt as if it was in her throat.

"Are we ready then, for the next line?" Da said gently, gladness showing in his eyes.

"Aye." Maureen glanced back at the fenced quarantine area. If Ma had come with them on this journey . . . No, she would not even let herself think it.

There were lines for money exchanging, lines to answer questions, lines to fill out papers. As she waited, Maureen listened to the many different languages being spoken. It was hard to believe people were actually saying something with all that gibberish. But then, even English sounded strange when spoken by the man at the money exchange.

At the last station Da was given an immigration paper with his name and the names of the children on it. "O.K., mister, you can go now," the official said, nodding toward the exits.

"You mean—?" Da looked about, uncertain of what to do.

"You got your papers, mister, move on!" The man shook his head impatiently. "O.K., now, who's next?" he shouted.

The O'Connors gathered up their belongings and trudged down the corridor leading to the exit gates. Da's papers were examined one more time and the gate was opened. All at once the family was standing alongside a busy street. Da walked a short distance, then set down his bundles. Maureen and the boys followed, their heads turning every which way, trying to see all things at once.

This was America. Horse-drawn wagons and pushcarts everywhere; people thick as fair time in Mallow. In the air the smell of hot tar, the sound of hammering. People coming and going as if the only business of the day was "Hurry!"

Maureen looked around. There were buildings in every direction as far as she could see. Her eyes searched for a small green field, or a stream like Allua Beg. Dust from a passing wagon rose in the air, clouding her view.

Da, too, was looking at the city. "We are here," he said. "Let us give thanks to God." Da prayed and asked a blessing on Ma, that she might soon join them. The city seemed quieter for a moment; then came the clatter of wheels again, and shouting.

Da dug in his pocket for the address from Kevin Mahoney. "Now, we need a place to lay our heads. Kevin thought Oliver Street not far from the docks. But I wonder which way?"

At that moment a square-built man with ruddy coloring came bounding over to Da as if he knew him. He put out his hand.

"Good afternoon to you, friend, may God bless you," he said. "You're one of my own, for it's myself that came from Ireland but two years ago."

The man shook Da's hand and gave Maureen a generous smile. "Aye, it's good to see such faces again. Well now, New York welcomes you, and Liam Carney does the same!"

"Thank you kindly," Da replied. "My name is Sean O'Connor. We've only just arrived." He held out the paper with the Oliver Street address. "Perhaps you could give me directions to this lodging house?"

Liam Carney squinted at the paper. "Oliver Street? Tsk, that's a long way off, surely. I couldn't be certain on the best way to get there." He tapped his chin thoughtfully. "But I've an idea, friend. There's a lodging house not far from here. I happen to know Mr. Lynch has a room to let this very day. If we hurry, I'm certain you could have it."

"But the rent? We've little money."

"Not to worry. Mr. Lynch is a good fellow; he'll understand."

Liam Carney leaned forward as if to speak confidentially. "And he has a grogshop below the rooms, where you might get a pint or two on the cuff as well."

Da glanced up at the sky. The sun was edging toward the horizon; in a few hours it would be dark. "If Mr. Lynch is a fair man, perhaps we're as well off lodging with him as on Oliver Street."

"I guarantee it." Liam Carney gave Da a friendly slap on the arm. "Here, let me help you with those bundles."

The man winked at Maureen and lifted the parcel she had been carrying. He turned and began striding up the street, leaving the others to hurry after him.

It was hard to take in all there was to see. Liam Carney

kept up a good pace, leading them down one street and up another. Maureen began to wonder what the man's notion of distance was, if the lodging house was "not far."

Brian pulled her arm. "Maureen, see there. That man has skin as dark as the peat."

It was true. A black man was wheeling a cart down the street, and two small children, as dark as the man himself, chased after him. Maureen's eyes widened.

"Faith, Brian, I never knew such could be."

The O'Connors were led on for several blocks. The streets became more cluttered, the buildings shabbier. It was near supper time and the smell of boiling cabbage wafted from open windows.

"Only a bit farther, lads," Liam Carney shouted to Brian and Paddy. Catching Maureen's eye, he winked at her again.

Maureen quickly looked down. The man made her uncomfortable; she wished Da had gone to Kevin's address instead.

Suddenly they came to a halt.

"Lynch's Grogshop, Lynch's Lodgings!" Carney threw out his arm, gesturing at an old three-story building. "Now, let's get you settled!"

He entered a doorway and began climbing the steep stairs. Da, Paddy, Brian and Maureen followed single file.

There was no light except what came in at the street level. By the time they reached the third floor, the stairs and landing were nearly in darkness.

Liam Carney led them down the shadowy hall and stopped before a half-open door. Lifting his foot, he kicked the door wide.

The room was tiny. A grimy window let in the last bit of the day's sunlight, just enough to reveal what Lynch's Lodgings had to offer.

39

Along one wall six bunks had been attached, and on each bunk was a thin gray mattress. Next to the bunks, the torn wallpaper hung in shreds. The only other furniture was a table; two boards propped across fruit boxes. Indeed, there was no space for anything else, as the black cookstove took up a good part of the room.

Maureen sniffed. There was an unpleasant odor that reminded her of the rats in the *Star*'s hold. Damp stains ran down one wall where rainwater had leaked in, and the floor was covered with trash. Maureen noticed animal droppings under the stove.

Da's face was glum as he looked around. Maureen could see his heart sinking. All those weeks on the *Star*, and now this.

"What amount, Mr. Carney, does the room let for?" Da asked.

"Ah now, I'm not sure. But Lynch won't be needing the money right away." Carney glanced around with satisfaction. "Well, you've your lodgings, but no supper. How about a meat pie, lads?" He grinned at Brian and Paddy.

"See here, Mr. Carney," Da said. "We've little money for meat pies and the like. We'll wait till morning and . . ."

"I won't hear of it; the food is on me. A man enjoys good company with his supper, eh?"

"But I don't want to be owing you."

Liam Carney held up his hand and winked at the boys. "Am I right, lads? It's time we ate? Now come along!" He stepped into the hallway.

Paddy moved eagerly forward, then stopped and looked back at his father.

Da let out his breath with a long sigh. He shrugged and gave a nod to Maureen and the boys. They followed Liam Carney down to the grogshop.

40

8
Fruit Vendors and a Chemist

Six weeks on the *Western Star* was a suitable introduction to Lynch's Lodgings. The building was damp, crowded, and dirty. It smelled badly. And George Lynch looked as flinty-eyed and mean-hearted as Mate Hawkins.

Also, the food in the grogshop was little better than the *Star*'s fare. Liam Carney's meat pies were heavy with fat; the grog was more water than rum.

But at least Maureen was able to bathe. It meant lugging a bucket of water from the pump in the yard, for she refused to wash in the midst of the drunken men who staggered from the grogshop.

Da spent the next day walking the streets inquiring for work. "No luck," he said when he returned. "There's plenty other men doing the same thing. Tomorrow will go better."

Maureen and the boys scouted the neighborhood, looking for a place to buy a bit of food and some tea. They found a street of open stalls where vendors sold vegetables and fruits. The produce was all in rows and lovely to see, but most things cost more than Maureen could pay. It was torture to see a stall of rosy plums and then buy only a small wilted cabbage.

Da set out again early the next morning. He had been told that digging crews near the river needed men, and he was going there first thing.

The previous day the boys had talked to a broom peddler, hoping he would hire them to help sell his wares. He had no need for assistants, but did tell them how they might gain a little food for the table.

"There be cast-offs from the produce vendors," he had said. "What they can't sell, they toss out. Be you nimble-footed, it's a decent prize you can fetch. But careful, lads, there be plenty competition."

So this morning Brian and Paddy headed down to the market stalls, making great talk between them of the pears and plums they'd be bringing back.

Maureen finished brushing her hair and tied it with a piece of yarn. There was simple pleasure in having a clean face again, and hair tidy. But the moldy smell of the ship's hold was still in her clothes; it mingled with the stale odors of smoke and grease wafting up from the grogshop.

She smoothed her skirt. Da had told her to seek out Mr. Lynch today and ask him the cost of the room. Until work was found, every penny must be carefully reckoned.

She went out, closing the door behind her. Each room in the lodging house held several tenants and a noisy hubbub came from the open doors. Most of the lodgers were men, and many were Irish. Da had recognized three of them as passengers from the *Star*.

As Maureen went down the stairs, she could hear a terrible commotion coming from one of the rooms on the second floor. A woman's voice, very angry, was shouting.

When Maureen reached the landing, the door to the room flew open and George Lynch, hands over his head, came running out. Behind him was a woman Maureen had seen in the grogshop. She was swinging at Mr. Lynch with a wooden beetle.

42

"Go live with the devil!" she cried. "Black-hearted miser!"

Mr. Lynch ducked his head and ran down the stairs. It was then the woman saw Maureen pressed up against the wall.

"Gracious goodness, I nearly landed this on you, girl." She looked down the stairwell as Mr. Lynch disappeared. "Oh, that evil man! And Liam Carney, too!"

Maureen blinked. "What is it they've done?"

The woman looked at Maureen more closely. "I've seen you before, haven't I? You live upstairs?"

"Aye."

"Then you'll be learning about Carney's tricks soon enough."

The words gave Maureen an uneasy feeling. "What is it you mean?"

"Did Liam Carney bring you here?"

"He did."

"Aye, him and his slippery tongue. Well, don't be thinking it was any favor. Lynch will take everything your da earns and give Carney half, same as he did with my Barry's pay."

"But Mr. Carney said—"

" 'Not to worry?' " The woman rolled her eyes. "You'll have worry enough when George Lynch wants what's owed him. Oh, he'll lead you on so's you trust him, but then he'll pounce. Move out today, before Lynch gets his hand in your pocket! Mind, the man is on friendly terms with the police, giving them free pints and all, so there's no use complaining to them."

Maureen looked around nervously. She hadn't liked Liam Carney from the first, but he was Irish and seemed willing to help Da. " 'Tis a low man who preys on his own people," she said.

"Aye, but greed is in him. 'Tis easy then to cheat

others, no matter who they are."

She turned toward her room. Maureen saw that there were tears in her eyes. "I've packing to do," the woman said, "for we'll not stay here one more night. Better to sleep in the streets." Then, with a sudden fierceness, she added, "May those men be soon cursed by a windy gallows!"

She closed her door and Maureen stood in the hallway alone, wondering what to do. She and Da and the boys would have to move to another lodging house. And soon, before they were more in debt to Mr. Lynch. Best, then, that she find Brian and Paddy and explain what was happening. Maureen went down the stairs quietly, slipping past the door of the grogshop and turning toward the marketplace.

It did not take her long to reach the produce stalls. The streets were crowded and Maureen felt a certain excitement being in the midst of so many people. Like the fair in Mallow it was, but not as festive. The greengrocers and fruit vendors shouted over one another and held out plums or oranges to the shoppers. Women with market baskets strolled along, their eyes sharp and noses working.

Passing a stall of ripe cherries, Maureen felt giddy with longing. If she was to search for her brothers among the fruit vendors, then someone had better tie her hands!

The boys were nowhere to be seen. Maureen decided to walk past the shops and look for them on that side of the street. She passed a dry goods store, a butcher, a display window of ladies' finery. These shops might need someone to sweep the floor or polish the glass, she thought. Perhaps tomorrow she could inquire.

The next shop was a chemist's with rows of colored bottles arrayed in the window. The door was ajar. Something caught her eye and she stepped closer to peer inside.

A small, white-haired man was bending over a stool on which a young boy sat. Blood oozed from the boy's nose and the man was laying a compress over it.

"Paddy!" Maureen called, running into the shop.

The man did not look up, but continued pressing the boy's nose. Paddy squirmed and tried to turn to Maureen.

Brian was sitting nearby on another stool. "Maureen, how did you find us?" he asked.

"I was only walking by! Whatever has happened?"

Before he could answer a door at the rear of the shop opened and a short, plump woman with silvery hair came out. She looked at Maureen and her eyes were bright with humor. "Who is this, Jacob?" she said.

"That's my sister," Paddy answered, jerking his head.

The man stepped back, scowling at Paddy. "You sit still. Keep your nose up, like I tell you before."

The man adjusted his glasses and carefully regarded Maureen. "Well? Are you here to collect these two ruffians?"

Maureen looked from Brian to Paddy.

"Ruffians? But what has happened?"

The woman came around the counter, her eyes noting Maureen's shabby dress and country brogans. "I am Mrs. Rothman," she said. "Are these two your brothers?"

"Aye. O'Connor is our name. Did Paddy fall?"

"I was only—" Paddy began, then stopped as blood trickled from his nose again.

"I can explain," said Brian, looking sheepishly at the chemist's wife. "We were down by the market, waiting for the cast-offs. Every time the food came our way, other lads got it. Then a large cabbage came flying by and Paddy caught it, jolly as you please. "Run!" he said to me, and we headed for the lodging house. But a gang of toughs gave

45

chase, saying we weren't allowed in the neighborhood. One of their big fellows grabbed Paddy and bloodied his nose, as you can see."

"At which time I am on my way home with a full shopping basket," Mrs. Rothman interrupted.

"Aye. Paddy got away and ran like the wind, except he didn't see Mrs. Rothman coming. Bang! Off went oranges, carrots and onions in every direction."

"And where am I?" asked Mrs. Rothman. "Flat on my back in the middle of Broome Street. But decent boys, these two. They helped me to my feet and returned all the goods to my basket."

"Not *all*," said Mr. Rothman. He lifted Paddy's shirt. Two carrots were stuffed inside the waist of the boy's pants.

"Oh, these," he mumbled, "I did forget."

"Tsk; you need more than carrots," Mrs. Rothman scolded. "Skin and bones, you are."

Maureen gave Paddy a dark look. "I'm very sorry for all this trouble," she said to Mrs. Rothman. " 'Twas kind of you to tend to Paddy's nose, and I thank you. We'll go now."

Mr. Rothman removed his eyeglasses and began polishing them. "The boy should sit a few minutes. No need to start that nose again."

"Jacob, tea and bread while they wait, eh?" Mrs. Rothman nudged her husband. "Come," she said to Maureen, "help with the kettle."

The room at the rear of the shop was small and cozy. It had a flowered rug, two chintz-covered chairs, a table with lace cloth and silver candleholder. Above the stove stood a row of shining crockery and against one wall were more books than Maureen had ever seen.

"All this, tucked behind a chemist's?" she said admiringly.

"Ah, but it seems empty now, for our daughter, Sarah, is away teaching school," Mrs. Rothman said.

"Your daughter is a teacher?" Maureen said with surprise. She thought of the young hedgemaster who sometimes traveled from village to village in Ireland. He was the only teacher she'd ever known.

Maureen carried a pot of tea and a plate of warm bread into the shop for Mrs. Rothman. Paddy nearly fell off his stool as Mrs. Rothman began serving.

"Mind your nose," Maureen said sternly.

A bell over the front door jingled and Mr. Rothman went to greet his customer.

"Nicholas, good afternoon."

"Jacob, the same. What have we here, a party?"

"One would think so. Anna, she likes to entertain." Mr. Rothman sorted through his bottles. "Ah, here is your medicine. And how is Else?"

"Better each day, thank you."

The chemist put a jar of amber liquid on the counter. "Fifteen cents it is, Nicholas."

"Eh . . . could I pay you on Friday, after I get my wages?"

Mr. Rothman wearily drew a notebook from under the counter. He thumbed past several pages, then stopped to write in a figure.

"I'm afraid there's still twenty cents left from last week."

"*Ja, ja,* I know, Jacob. You'll get it *all* on Friday. I won't forget."

Mr. Rothman nodded and closed the book. "Very well. Friday. Certain."

"Ah, thank you, Jacob! Good day to you. And to you, Anna." The man tipped his hat and hurried out the door.

Mr. Rothman's eyeglasses slipped down again as he came back to his teacup.

"Today I fix a boy's nose after he steals my wife's carrots.

47

I give credit to a man who never pays me. Am I some sort of fool?"

"Jacob, hush." His wife poked him. Then, gently, she said, "Your tea, it's gone cold. Let me warm it."

Maureen cleared her throat. "Thank you for the bread and tea, ma'am," she said. " 'Twas very good. But we'll not be troubling you any more." She crooked a finger at Brian and Paddy. "Come along, boys."

Mrs. Rothman swept the bread crumbs into her hand. "You're no trouble. I enjoy a bit of company. Though I could do without the spill on Broome Street next time."

Paddy hopped down from the stool and gingerly touched his nose.

"It's still there," the chemist told him. "But don't go using it to hit the knuckles of the boys in the neighborhood."

"No, sir, I won't." Paddy smiled at Mrs. Rothman. "Thank you, ma'am, for your fine eats!"

Brian was over near the jars of medicine, reading the labels. "Laudanum, camphor, horehound, arrow—"

"Brian," Maureen called. "We are going."

"All right, I'm coming." He nodded at the Rothmans. "Good day, then, and thank you kindly for the tea and bread." He followed Maureen out the door.

The three walked the length of the block in silence. Finally Maureen spoke.

"Well. Lucky you were, Paddy. Next time, no fighting!"

"*We* weren't fighting, they were."

"Still. And more politeness to the chemist and his wife. They were good to you."

As they turned off Broome Street, Maureen stopped walking. "Boys. Before we get back to the lodging house . . . I have to tell you something. That man, Carney, and Mr. Lynch, they're up to no good."

"What do you mean? Mr. Carney bought us meat pies."

"Aye. That's all part of it, to put us in mind of his generous nature. But listen."

Maureen told them what had happened that morning and neither boy said anything for a few minutes. Brian's face was solemn. Paddy's mouth screwed up, working over what Maureen had told them. He looked angry.

"Boys, maybe we can move out right away, go someplace else. We'll tell Da as soon as he gets back."

Da was already at the lodging house when Maureen and the boys arrived. Maureen knew from the look of him that he'd not found any work. Then she noticed the family's belongings were tied into bundles.

"Da," she began. "That man Carney, he—"

Da held up his hand. "I already know. I was at the Hibernian Brotherhood today. Carney's name, and Lynch's, too, are well-known down there. Carney's a 'shoulder-hitter,' a man with a ready smile but a hand to steal from your pocket."

"I saw Kevin Mahoney at the Brotherhood office too. He said Mrs. Duffy's room on Oliver Street is still available. We're going there tonight."

Maureen shivered. "Sneak out of here, will we?"

"Aye. With not a word of noise."

"But, Da, what about the people arriving on boats tomorrow and the next day? Carney will have them in our place," Brian said.

"Not for long, my son. The Brotherhood is posting men to take care of 'shoulder-hitters.' And Mr. Lynch will do little business when his ale kegs are split open."

The hour grew late. Da listened. Voices could still be heard down in the grogshop, but they were the voices of men who had taken too many pints, men unlikely to hear footsteps creeping down the stairs.

49

Good. It was time, then.

"Ready?"

"Aye."

"Carney said the pies were his treat. So they will be."
Da put a coin on the table. "Here's two days rent for Mr.
Lynch, the greedy stoat. He can't say I didn't pay." The
coin reflected dully in the pale moonlight that came
through the window.

"And both men can go to the devil," Da muttered.

The bundles were made secure. Maureen went down
the stairs first. If anyone saw her, she would say she was
getting a bit of air. At her safe signal, Da and the boys
would follow.

All went well. They rounded the corner from Lynch's
Lodgings and paused to rearrange their baggage.

"Away on!" Da whispered, and their footsteps echoed
on the dark cobblestones.

9
Oliver Street

The neighborhood surrounding Oliver Street was shabby. Once-proud dwellings had been converted into cramped lodging houses; leaky sheds and windowless cellars were now "rooms-to-let." Yet tall elm trees, leafy with summer, lined the street, and in the moonlight Maureen could see flower boxes in many of the windows.

Da stopped in front of a narrow row house. "This is the number Kevin gave me. I wonder is Mrs. Duffy still up?"

He stepped to the door but before he could knock the door opened. A plain-looking woman with solemn eyes and a tired face stood there. "O'Connor, is it?" she said.

"Aye. Kevin Mahoney sent me."

"I'm Nora Duffy."

She smiled then, only a little, but with a look that took in Da's frayed jacket, the boys' smudged faces, Maureen's "old country" shawl.

"Third floor, it is," Mrs. Duffy said as she led them up the stairs. "The only room left." She held out a lamp and opened a door at the end of the hall.

The room was not much bigger than the one at Lynch's. It had the same sagging bunks, board-and-box table, black cookstove. But the wallpaper was in place, curtains hung in the window, and someone had taken the trouble to sweep the floor.

"The rent is one dollar fifteen cents the week," Mrs. Duffy said, "including wood for the stove. The wood is out back, next to the privy."

Da nodded.

"The rent is paid in advance," Mrs. Duffy added.

"Ah," Da said, reaching into his pocket. He drew out his money, counted it, frowned, and counted again. "Dollars, pounds, I have trouble with the difference," he apologized. He looked at Mrs. Duffy. "I've not found work yet, and we've no food. Kevin and I are going to the gas works tomorrow; he says it's sure they'll hire us. Could I pay half the rent now, and the rest when I've my wages?"

Mrs. Duffy folded her arms. "Aye, that will do."

Da smiled broadly and gave her the money. "I'm grateful, Mrs. Duffy."

The woman turned to Maureen. "The stale-bread man comes by at half-eight each morning. You can get a decent loaf for a few pennies."

"I'll see to it."

"Knock on my door afterwards and I'll tell you about the shops, who's pricey and all."

"I will. Thank you kindly."

Mrs. Duffy said good night. Her footsteps sounded heavy on the stairs as she departed.

Maureen took Da's hand. "She's much nicer than old Lynch."

"Aye, daughter. There's a good woman, I'm thinking."

Maureen surveyed the family's new lodging. Although it was small, there was no moldy smell nor sign of rodents. With a bit of effort it could be a decent home.

Paddy and Brian were standing by the open window,

looking down at the dark street. Paddy leaned his head out, making a hawking sound as he gathered saliva from his throat. All at once he let go a mouthful of spit, sending it out in a wide arc.

"Hey, Brian," he said, "I almost hit the lamppost. Now you try."

Maureen reeled about. "Will you have some manners?" she scolded. "Mrs. Duffy will think us common trash."

"Heed your sister, boys," Da said.

Paddy made a face. "Nobody's out at this hour. 'Twas no harm done."

Maureen pointed to the blankets. "No? Well, I say better you give a hand to making up these beds."

Da and Kevin hoped to be first in line at the gas works and were gone before sunup.

Maureen rose and began sorting through the family belongings. First out were teapot and kettle. Then the crucifix from Ma and a vial of holy water. "Perhaps now we've a proper place for these things," she murmured, looking up at the wall.

Somewhere up the street church bells were tolling eight o'clock. Maureen told the boys to keep watch at the window for Mrs. Duffy's stale-bread man.

A stream of peddlers and delivery wagons began wending its way down Oliver Street. From their vantage point the boys had a good view of the traffic. A man pushing a large cart moved slowly down the block and at every doorway someone stopped him to make a purchase.

"Maureen, I think 'tis the bread man!" Brian called.

Maureen glanced quickly out the window. "Aye, that must be him." She felt in her pocket for the pennies and ran out the door.

By the time she reached the street several people were

crowding around the bread cart. Maureen stood on tiptoe and eyed the bread. The loaves were long and crusty, dark at the edges but promising to be soft inside. Her mouth watered.

Behind her, a woman began pushing forward.

"Begging your pardon?" Maureen said with a glare. She planted her feet firmly and held fast to the cart.

"Leo, a nice rye, if you please," someone called out.

"Have you egg bread today?"

"Ah, Leo darlin', three Viennas for Mrs. Riley."

"That one, please, with the poppy seeds."

The stack of bread was shrinking rapidly. Maureen paused, then suddenly called out: "Leo, have you a wheaten loaf?"

Leo turned and looked at her. "Oh, wheaten is it? 'Wheaten, sweeten, we're down by the river meetin'?"

The other women looked at Maureen with amusement. "Not to tease, Leo, not to tease," one of them said to the bread man.

"Wheaten, it is." He smiled and plucked a large brown loaf from the pile, then handed it to Maureen. "Four cents, young miss."

Maureen counted out the money. "Thank you," she said, "and a good day to you." She tucked the bread under her arm. It was a solid loaf and she felt pleased with the purchase.

Maureen waved at the boys, holding the bread up so they could see it. Paddy opened the door as she came up the stairs. The bread knife was in his hand, ready.

"Easy, boy," Maureen said. "This bread is also for tonight, and Da. *I'll* cut it."

The bread was indeed stale, but had a good, nutty taste. The boys wolfed down their pieces and begged for more.

"I would risk this old nose for a cup of tea," Paddy sighed, licking the crumbs from his hand.

"Aye." Maureen looked at the teapot sitting on the stove. "I'll ask Mrs. Duffy where we might buy some, though we've little money left."

"Brian and I are going about the neighborhood today, to see does anyone have a job for us, or need errands run," Paddy said.

"Maybe we'll water and groom the peddler's horses," Brian added.

"That ought to be worth a few pennies."

Maureen regarded Paddy closely. "Mind, though, not another fray."

"Sure, no, Maureen." Paddy looked at her innocently.

The boys went out and turned up the street. Maureen stopped at Mrs. Duffy's door and knocked twice. There was no answer. She was about to knock again when the door opened and a bleary-eyed man peered out.

"Whaddaya want?" he said, his voice clogged with sleep.

"Is . . . is Mrs. Duffy in?"

"Upondaruf."

"What?"

"Upondaruf. Da ruf." The man closed his eyes and shut the door in Maureen's face.

"Oh, bother," Maureen muttered to herself. What did he mean, "da ruf?" Wait. The roof? That ladder at the end of the hall; Paddy said it led to the roof. Mrs. Duffy was up on the roof?

Maureen lifted her skirt and hurried up the stairs. She would soon find out.

The ladder ended at a trapdoor in the ceiling. The door gave easily and Maureen poked her head up through the

opening. Sure enough, there was Mrs. Duffy, bending over a row of flat boxes.

"Good morning, Mrs. Duffy," Maureen called.

Mrs. Duffy straightened her back and squinted at Maureen. "Oh, it's you, girl. Good morning." She was holding a market basket filled with dark green leaves.

"Is that mint?" Maureen asked, catching the sharp freshness of the herb.

"Aye, and wilting in this hot sun."

Maureen saw that mint was growing from several boxes on the roof. " 'Tis a great lot of mint," she said.

Mrs. Duffy laughed. "It is, that. I sell it to restaurants and the like. Oh, there's not a lot of money to be made, but it adds to what I get for running the lodging house."

Maureen looked around. Rooftops of other buildings extended in all directions. Blackened chimneys stood midst the white sheets that flapped from clotheslines. Overhead, two pigeons eyed Mrs. Duffy, hoping for a toss of bread crumbs.

" 'Tis lovely up here," Maureen said, feeling the breeze lift her hair. Off in the distance, the blue of the water came up to the horizon. She thought of the young sailor from the *Western Star.* No doubt he was out there now, somewhere on that wide ocean.

"Aye, it's peaceful on the rooftops," said Mrs. Duffy. "How did you know I was up here?"

"A man downstairs told me."

"Mick, that was. My husband. Just back last night from a long journey, and having no sleep."

"I'm sorry I woke him. I wanted to ask you about the shops."

"Of course." Mrs. Duffy covered the mint sprigs with a cloth. "What is your name, girl?"

"Maureen."

"Aye. Well then, Maureen, Mr. Pike, the tea merchant, is a fair man. He's over on Henry Street. Farther down is Maguire the grocer. Now Mrs. Maguire is a tight fist, but she'll not cheat you. Should you go into Kelly the draper's, mind you keep an eye on your pennies, for he'll turn your head with his pretty ribbons and such."

"Mr. Pike's on Henry," Maureen repeated. "And Maguire's . . ." She paused. "Do you know, Mrs. Duffy, of a shop that might be hiring a girl like myself?"

Mrs. Duffy thought a moment. "Not around here. The families that run the shops have plenty of help, what with their own children and other relatives."

"Are there shops elsewhere? Perhaps a bakery, or . . . or a sweet shop?" Maureen's face brightened.

Mrs. Duffy smiled and patted her basket of mint. "Oh, girl, 'tis a dreamer you be." The woman looked out over the rooftops and her expression grew solemn. " 'Tis sometimes hard for new folks to find work. Especially now, with so many coming off the boats each day."

Maureen frowned. "But I'd not be any trouble. Sure I'm a hard enough worker."

"Aye." Mrs. Duffy pointed to a red brick building several blocks away. "See over yonder, where the two chimneys are side by side? Now you might try there. 'Tis the match factory. Early each morning they hire girls and women for the day."

Maureen had in mind the shop window she'd seen yesterday, the one with a display of ladies' finery. But perhaps she would give Mrs. Duffy's suggestion a try.

10
A Trip to the Match Factory

Da was in good spirits that night. He and Kevin had been hired as laborers at the gas works. " 'Tis only a day's work at a time," Da said, "and the pay's not much. But 'tis a start." He reached into his jacket and took out three small sausages. "Here, Maureen, cook these. They're for you and the boys. And I've a pint of milk as well."

Maureen quickly got out the iron skillet. She had bought a small amount of tea from Mr. Pike and while the sausages were cooking she sliced the remaining bread to have with a fresh pot of tea.

Da smiled as he looked at the table's modest but appetizing fare. "This room, 'tis beginning to seem a real home," he said.

At that moment Brian and Paddy came in the door. "Is that sausage I'm smelling?" asked Paddy, rushing to the table.

"Aye," Da answered, pleased. "Wash up now, boys. There's a good supper waiting."

Both Maureen and Da were up before sunrise. "Good luck at the hiring line," Da said as he put on his jacket. He patted Maureen's arm and quietly opened the door, taking care not to waken the sleeping boys. "Soon we'll all be working and can save up for Ma's fare."

"Aye," Maureen replied. "Good-by, Da. Good luck to you, as well."

Maureen finished brushing her hair, then grabbed her shawl and hurried down the stairs. She did not want to be late getting to the match factory.

A chill fog had come off the river and now hung on the morning air. Maureen shivered and moved closer into the crowd waiting for the factory to open. The building was a dull red structure and reminded Maureen of the poorhouse in Ballyvourney. "Perhaps I'll be lucky today," she thought, looking around. The match factory was said to pay eight cents an hour and the hope of such earnings had brought many young women to the loading dock.

"Rosie, you've been hired here before, haven't you?" someone asked the woman standing next to Maureen.

"I was," Rosie answered, "But not likely I'll be chosen again. Got into a scrap, I did."

"What happened?"

Rosie tossed back her hair. "Some hussy wouldn't let me into the privy. 'You Irish are too dirty,' she said. 'Go use the bushes.' "

Maureen frowned. "What did you do?"

"Sure weren't all the other workers watching, hoping for a fray? So I said, 'If I'm dirty, miss, it's from working too close to the likes of you. Maybe this will help you clean yourself.' And I spit in her face!"

Maureen gasped, then burst into laughter. Several nearby women poked at Rosie good-naturedly.

A man's voice from the dock caught the crowd's attention. "You there, and you," the foreman said, pointing his long stick at the women. "Yeah, you . . . and you . . ."

Maureen stood on tiptoe, hoping the man would see

her. He reached the count of thirty and stopped. "The rest, come back tomorrow. Maybe I can take more then."

"*Och,* bad cess to him," Maureen muttered, watching the foreman summoning the day's workers into the factory. "Why couldn't he have taken a few more?" She folded her arms in a dejected manner.

Rosie was also looking up at the dock. "See? He didn't pick a single Irish girl. Not one of us has been hired all week."

Another woman nodded. " 'Tis no use coming here anymore."

"Just as well, I say," commented Rosie. "The neighbor upstairs told me you get a terrible sickness from working in match factories. Eats away your face!"

"No, Rosie. How could there be such?"

"I don't know. But this woman swears 'tis true. 'Phossy jaw,' it's called. Her own sister has it; she's so ugly now she won't go outside."

Maureen grimaced. "But those women all seemed . . ."

"Aw, you have to be around the stuff a while before something bad happens. Anyway, who cares? Let them have their old matches." Rosie waved her hand and went on up the street.

Maureen stood on the corner, uncertain of what to do now. Perhaps the match factory was a disagreeable place, but she would have been pleased to tell Da that she had found work there today.

11
Letter from America

August 1, 1847

My dearest Mary,

It was my hope that when this letter came to be written, I could tell you of our good fortune in America. But fortune does not come easy, even here. Jobs are scarce now, for hundreds like myself are coming off the boats each week. I have done digging and hod-carrying, but none of it steady. Men talk of better luck in coal mines further west, where there is work every day and good wages.

Our home is a small room in a lodging house, set down in a city of so many people, I look about in wonder. Maureen cares for her brothers and myself, and the boys help their da as best they can. But it is lonely without you, dear cushla.

I hope you are getting stronger and that Owen and his family are well. Tell your brother that if the streets in America are made of gold, I have yet to find any.

How I long for the day we will be together again. Father Murphy of St. Brendan's, who has kindly helped me write this letter, prays at every Mass for the families in Ireland.

You are in my thoughts each night, and my heart forever.

Your devoted husband,
Sean Padraic O'Connor

12
Honest Work

Da and Kevin Mahoney sat opposite each other at the table. Both men looked tired and in need of a good wash. Kevin drew a whiskey bottle from his pocket and offered it to Da.

Da took a swig and set the bottle down. "Pig sweat," he said, wrinkling his nose.

Kevin shrugged and tipped the bottle back, taking a long swallow. "Better than nothing at all," he said with a wipe to his mouth.

"So, Kevin," Da said. "Pennsylvania, is it, and the coal mines?"

"Aye. There's nothing in New York anymore for the likes of us."

Maureen, Brian and Paddy stood nearby, listening. If Kevin went to work in the coal mines, would Da go, too? It had been three weeks since he'd been laid off at the gas works, and he'd had no other employment.

"Sean, I've talked to that fellow Morgan," Kevin continued. "He's nearly got a crew ready. We can start next week. I'm figuring to save a lot of money out there, what with the high wages and the company giving us lodgings."

Da shook his head. "If only we could have stayed at the gas works. Curse that foreman! We worked as hard as any man there."

Kevin took another swallow of the whiskey. "*Och,* it was no accident when that load fell on you our last day. Lucky you weren't killed, Sean."

Da rubbed a lump at the back of his head. "I expect you're right."

"Those other men didn't want us around. 'Get rid o' the micks,' they told the foreman. It's the same everywhere and I'm tired of it."

Da began pacing back and forth. "But what have we done? Is it a crime to be asking for honest work?"

"It's 'cause we're Catholics," said Paddy.

Da turned and looked at him. "Who told you that?"

"Whacker Nolan. He showed me a bunch o' signs down the Bowery. Somebody's written 'No Irish Here,' and 'Kick the Pope.' Whacker says the Irish have to stick together in America, same as fighting the English back home."

"And who is this Whacker?" Da wanted to know.

"He's a friend o' mine. And he knows a lot of the big swells from uptown, politicians and the like. I help him sell his newspapers. Whacker says he'll get me my own corner soon."

Kevin took a long drink from the bottle. "Paddy's friend is right about one thing; we need to stick together. The Brotherhood says when all of us start voting, the politicians will come down here and pay attention."

Da resumed his pacing. "I don't know about that, but if it wasn't for Nora Duffy, I'd be out on the street now. I can't keep this up much longer."

"Come to Pennsylvania, Sean, work the coal!" Kevin glanced at Maureen and the boys. "The children . . . they'll be all right here. You can send them money."

63

There was strong urging in Kevin's voice.

Da stopped at the window. His shoulders sagged and he shook his head wearily as he looked down at the dark street. It was a long time before he spoke.

"Maureen, could you manage things . . . if I were to leave?"

"Aye, Da." She tried to sound confident.

"Boys? You'd not be giving me any worry, nor your sister, either?"

"No, Da," in unison.

"Then . . . I'm for having a try at Pennsylvania. I'll speak to Mrs. Duffy about it in the morning."

The room on Oliver Street seemed empty with Da gone. Maureen missed seeing his jacket on the wall peg and his muddy brogans lying under the bunk. She found herself listening for his voice coming up the stairs at the end of the day, and then remembered that he would not be home.

She arose early each morning in order to make the rounds of the hiring lines: first to the domestic service hall, then across to the sausage works, and last, to the match factory. Two days in a row she had been sent up to Gotham Court to clean a dormitory building that had caught fire. The owner was anxious to get in his paying tenants and as soon as the tiny rooms were cleared of rubble he dismissed the cleaning crew. Maureen took her earnings and left, glad to be out of the rotten dwelling. She had feared that at any moment it might collapse around her.

She was feeling discouraged as she went up on the roof to help Mrs. Duffy cut mint. It might be weeks before money from Da arrived, and the merchants on Henry Street were growing impatient. They were not as understanding as Mrs. Duffy regarding debts.

Mrs. Duffy tried to explain why it was difficult for immigrants to find decent work in New York. "Look at the Americans, Maureen. They don't want someone taking their jobs and putting them on the street. Of course, when a boatload of hungry Irish arrive, willing to work for half-pay, the bosses smell extra profit. So they let the regular workers go. Then there's fighting and trouble sure. It gives the Irish a bad name."

Mrs. Duffy's words bothered Maureen. It seemed as if Ireland's troubles had followed her to America.

"Mrs. Duffy, do you know who threw paint all over the walls down on the Bowery?"

Mrs. Duffy scowled. "Oh, the same crowd that chased Father Murphy last week. Fools with nothing better to do. I've seen them bother the Jews the same way, taking after a man for his religion, calling him names."

"By the way, Maureen," said Mrs. Duffy, "I told your da I'd try to find someone to share the room, to help you on the rent. There's a man coming round tonight, a Mr. O'Leary, and I think he's just the right fellow. He works down at the knackers, and has a family in Ireland waiting to join him."

"The knackers?"

"The glue factory. 'Tis a smelly place, and poor Mr. O'Leary announces himself long before he comes into view."

"Well, better a foul smell than to be down some dark coal mine, I'm thinking."

Maureen went near the rooftop's edge and looked over. She could see all the way to Henry Street and it was pleasant to view the activities below from this quiet vantage point.

Mrs. Duffy came and stood beside her. "A peaceful spot, this rooftop," she said. "Look, Maureen, isn't that your Brian coming round the corner?"

Maureen leaned forward. "Aye, and he seems in a hurry." She waved her arms to catch the boy's attention. "Oh, Brian, up here!"

Brian heard his name and stopped. Puzzled, he turned one way and then the other. Maureen called again and he looked up, a grin spreading across his face. "Maureen!" he shouted, "I've a job at the chemist's!"

"What's that?" Maureen shouted back. "The chemist's?"

Brian repeated the news but the wind caught his words and Maureen could not hear them. He came on up the street and ran into the lodging house. A few minutes later his head poked through the trapdoor.

"I've a job with Mr. Rothman," he said, scrambling onto the roof and coming over to Maureen and Mrs. Duffy. "I'm on my way to Mr. Pike's now, to deliver his medicine." Brian patted a small bottle protruding from his pocket.

"Brian, that's grand," said Maureen. "Will you work every day?"

"Aye. Running messages, sweeping, washing up and the like. Maureen, you should see all the books the Rothmans have."

"Oh, I remember from the day with Paddy's nose."

"Mrs. Rothman said I can read them, too, so long as I take care." Brian smiled. "That Mr. Rothman is a curious sort. 'No rest for your feet if you work for me,' he says, with a frown black as thunder. Then first thing he does is send me back to the missus for bread and jam."

"Oh, Brian, aren't you our lucky old goat?" Maureen gave her brother an affectionate pat.

"Huh. I'd better be off to Mr. Pike's now. He'll be wanting his camphor."

"Good-by then, boy-o. I'll see you later."

Maureen smiled to herself. Wouldn't Brian be the one to get himself a job with books and tea right there waiting? If only Paddy could do the same. But Paddy did have the newspapers and his own corner on which to hawk them now. And proud he was, to finally be a part of Whacker Nolan's gang. It had meant a few more bloody noses to prove himself, but Paddy had not complained. Maureen wasn't quite sure about Whacker Nolan. He was a rough sort whose loud manner was well-known in the neighborhood. Yet he seemed to get on well with the merchants, and Maureen had even seen him talking to Father Murphy on occasion. He struck her as being a bit shifty-eyed was all, and not a man with whom she was comfortable.

That evening Mrs. Duffy came by with the new lodger. What she had said about Mr. O'Leary was true: the foul smell of the knackers traveled with him. He apologized for this and assured Maureen that he would launder his clothes frequently.

Mr. O'Leary was a spare man, bent in the shoulders and with a habit of leaning forward, eyebrows raised, as if he didn't quite hear what was being said. He had a wife and five children living in Enniskerry and planned to send for them as soon as he had the money.

"The country is in ruin," he said, his voice sick with longing. "Sometimes I think the English would have us all dead, and use Ireland for pasture only."

Mr. O'Leary began unpacking his belongings. Two books immediately caught Brian's attention.

"*The Battle of Clontarf*, is it?" the boy asked, eyeing the first book.

"Ah, are you familiar with the great Brian Boru?" asked Mr. O'Leary.

"I am, indeed."

Mr. O'Leary seemed pleased. "Here then, have a look while I settle my things."

Soon Mr. O'Leary and Brian were talking of Brian Boru's victory over the Vikings at Clontarf. Also in Mr. O'Leary's pack was a book of Irish bards which he promised to share with the boy. Maureen could see that the smell of the knackers was quickly forgiven as far as Brian was concerned.

There was a sound of footsteps coming up the stairs and in a moment Paddy came in the door struggling with a large burlap sack. "Brian, give a hand," he said, "before I lose these apples."

Brian helped lay the sack on the table and several bright red apples tumbled out.

"Oh, Paddy, those are lovely," Maureen said. "Sure the huckster was asking a dear price for the very same today."

Paddy shrugged. "Whacker got 'em for me. He can get stuff on the cheap 'cause he knows everybody."

Maureen picked up an apple. It was firm and smelled crisply of autumn. "Then . . . they're ours to eat?"

Paddy scratched his chin in a way that imitated Da with his beard. He cocked his head at her. "Aye, Maureen, they're to eat. You don't think I brought 'em home just to look at?"

Maureen suddenly remembered Mr. O'Leary. "Oh, Paddy, I forgot. This is Mr. O'Leary. He's going to be lodging with us till Da returns."

Paddy looked at the man. Mr. O'Leary smiled and held out his hand. "Hello, lad. Are you as fond of the books as your brother?"

Paddy shook Mr. O'Leary's hand. "No, I'm not. But I read *The Irish Messenger* every day."

"The newspaper?"

"Aye. I help sell it, too. If you'd be wanting a copy, I

68

can get one for you."

Mr. O'Leary nodded. "That's good of you. I sometimes read the *Messenger* when I'm in at Larkin's."

Paddy withdrew a small knife from his pocket. He unsheathed it and began cutting into an apple. Maureen peered over his shoulder to get a closer look.

" 'Tis a new knife, Paddy? Sure Da didn't leave such behind, did he?"

Paddy kept his eyes on the apple as he cored it. "No. 'Twas in the alley behind Larkin's. I found it amongst the bushes."

"Oh. I see."

Mr. O'Leary smiled apologetically. "Maureen, boys. I'm afraid I must be going to bed now; my shift at the knackers starts at half-six."

"Of course," said Maureen. " 'Tis time for all of us to sleep, I'm thinking."

Mr. O'Leary began making up his bed in the corner alcove. "Have you employment, Maureen?"

"Ah, no. I can't seem to get on anywhere."

"I'll keep an eye out for jobs when I'm running errands for Mr. Rothman," offered Brian.

"Huh? Mr. Rothman?" asked Paddy.

"He's taken me on as shop boy. I started today."

"Why you wanna work for him, Brian?"

"He asked me. Or rather, his wife did. I get to read their books, too."

"Huh," Paddy said again. "Me, I'd rather be with the Irish; fellows like Whacker. We'll be in with his friend Mr. Dooley soon, and Dooley's important."

Brian frowned. "I don't mind working for the Rothmans. They're decent folk."

"Aye, they are," replied Paddy. "Still, better to be with your own kind, if you ask me."

69

13
The Hard Road

Maureen took a deep breath and went into Maguire's Grocery. Oh, good luck! Mrs. Maguire was in the back and Katy was minding the counter.

"Good morning, Katy," Maureen said softly, hoping Mrs. Maguire wouldn't hear. "Could I have one pound of flour and two of oats, please?"

Katy Maguire was chewing on a licorice stick. The open tin of licorice sat on the counter next to jars of toffee, fruit drops, and broken chocolate. Katy bent over the flour bins and Maureen's eyes fastened on the sweets. The open tin of licorice taunted her.

"There you be," Katy said, putting the flour and oats into Maureen's basket. "Anything else today?"

Maureen looked at the licorice juice dribbling down Katy's chin. "Ah . . . no," she said. "You'll put this on our account?"

Katy nodded and opened the ledger book, at the same time reaching for another piece of candy. "I will, Maureen, but Ma says you have to start paying soon."

"Oh, I will! As soon as I—"

"—'get money from my da.' I know." Katy sounded bored.

Maureen took her basket and went to the door. "Thank you," she said curtly. "Tell your ma I'll pay something next week, certain."

Maureen walked quickly back toward the lodging house. "That was a foolish thing to say," she muttered. "What will you pay her with, ashes from the stove?"

Old Sal, the blind peddler, was coming along the street pushing her cart of woven doormats. She reached down and patted her dog, who began wagging his tail at Maureen.

"Who's that comin', Barney?" asked Old Sal, leaning to one side. "That Maureen, is it?"

"Good morning to you, Old Sal," Maureen said. It amazed her that the blind woman always recognized her, even before she spoke.

"Mornin' to you, girl. There's fall in the air."

"Aye, that's so."

"Get your knittin' needles out, Maureen. You be wanting mittens soon enough." Old Sal chuckled. " 'Less you get a man to keep your hands warm."

"Go on with your talk," laughed Maureen. "I'll not be getting any man."

Old Sal moved slowly up the street, smiling to herself and humming. Barney stayed close beside her.

Maureen noticed that the trees on Henry Street were beginning to change color. Old Sal was right, the weather would soon turn cold, and warmer clothing would be needed.

Nora Duffy was sweeping the stoop when Maureen reached Oliver Street. As soon as she saw Maureen, she motioned at her to hurry.

"I hoped you'd be along! I've urgent business over on Jackson, and need help carrying some things. Could you come with me?"

"Oh, aye, Mrs. Duffy. Right now?"

"I've still a seedy-cake to wrap. Come along inside, it will take a minute."

They went into Mrs. Duffy's room. Maureen had not seen Mr. Duffy in weeks, and there was no sign of him today. A large traveling bag lay on the floor, and a caraway seed cake sat cooling on the table.

"Oh, my. 'Tis a lovely sight," Maureen said, eyeing the round cake. "My ma used to make seedy-cake."

"A balm for every woe, it is," Mrs. Duffy said with a faint smile as she wrapped the cake and carefully lowered it into a wicker basket. She slung a bag over one arm and held the wicker basket in the other.

"If you'll take the satchel there, Maureen, we'll be off."

Maureen lifted the traveling bag. It was heavy and felt of clothes and shoes. "Ready," she said.

Nora Duffy strode briskly along and Maureen had to hurry to keep up. They had crossed Market and were well down Monroe Street before Mrs. Duffy said anything.

"It's not only the Irish that have had their freedom stolen from them."

Maureen looked up, startled by the remark and by the heat in Mrs. Duffy's voice.

"The black folks who are slaves," Mrs. Duffy said, tightening her jaw, "they've suffered terribly."

Maureen had heard of slavery. Not in New York, but far away, in what was called "the South." It had puzzled her. There were black people right here in the neighborhood who were the same as anyone else. She knew some of them: Hickory, the iceman, and Old Sal, the blind woman over on Henry Street.

Mrs. Duffy clicked her tongue. "Slaves work the land while the owners grow rich. Just like your da giving his crops to the English landlord year after year, and himself staying poor as ever."

Maureen thought a moment. "I heard Mr. Pike say that slaves are well cared for, with cottages to live in, and food and clothes provided. That's better than any landlord would do."

Mrs. Duffy smiled wearily. "But what if your da was owned by another man, bought and sold like a dumb animal? A slave is fed and sheltered, that's true. But so is a workhorse. You'd not wish to trade places with one, I'll wager."

Maureen had never given the matter much thought. Slavery was something far away, and besides, didn't she have her own worries?

"Why do some places allow slaves?" she asked. "What about the black people in New York?"

"Some have never been slaves. Others . . . have escaped, run away from their masters to a free state." Mrs. Duffy looked uneasily over her shoulder. "Slavery started in this country a long time ago, Maureen, and it profits certain men. You know, greed is not just an English disease."

They were nearing the East River where the neighborhood was filled with warehouses. Mrs. Duffy stopped before an old building on Jackson Street.

"Maureen, the business I have here; it's personal. You'll not mind waiting outside?

"Ah, no."

Mrs. Duffy took the traveling bag. "I'll try to hurry."

Maureen felt some disappointment. Good-by to the seedy-cake and any chance of sampling it. She sat down on the step to wait, wondering who Mrs. Duffy could be visiting.

She thought about what Mrs. Duffy had said regarding slavery. It was true that she wouldn't want Da to be a slave, even if it did mean food and clothes and a place to live.

A few minutes later Mrs. Duffy called from the building. Her voice was tense.

"Maureen, come in here!"

Maureen jumped up and stepped carefully through the debris that littered the walk. The building was dark inside and it was hard to see where she was going.

"This way, hurry!" Mrs. Duffy was at the end of the hall. She pushed open a sagging door. No one was in the room, but Maureen could hear muffled voices coming from somewhere. Nail kegs were stacked against one wall, and odd pieces of lumber lay here and there. The room must have once been a carpenter's work place.

Mrs. Duffy moved a sawhorse to one side. Behind it was a door, barely noticeable in the dim light. She rapped twice and the door was opened by a middle-aged woman who gave Maureen a quick, appraising look.

The room they entered was long and narrow, with rows of shelves similar to a supply closet. Maureen looked around. She gasped and stepped back, sickened by what she saw. A black man lay on the floor, his contorted face turned toward her. One of his legs was a raw, open wound, nearly severed at the knee. Another black man knelt beside him, cradling the injured man's head in his lap.

Nearby stood a sober-looking white man in a well-tailored suit. He turned to the woman who had opened the door.

"I'm sorry, Miss Trump," he said. "But that leg must come off. Otherwise, he hasn't a chance."

"Can thee do it here, Doctor?" the woman asked in a low voice. "Their master has trailed them all the way from Georgia. He'll be checking every hospital, for he knows Amos is badly injured. He means to take them back, as a lesson to the others."

The doctor removed his pince-nez and held it up to the

kerosene lamp. He took out a handkerchief and began to polish the lenses.

Mrs. Duffy stepped forward. "We have the money to pay you, Dr. Barnes, if that will hurry your decision."

"Now, Mrs. Duffy, I'm only considering the man's welfare. There's great risk, doing an amputation in a place such as this. However, with some assistance, it can be done."

"Maureen." Mrs. Duffy's voice brought Maureen to attention. "There's a pump out back and a stove down the hall. Fill those two buckets and heat the water to boiling. Hurry!"

"I'll want wrappings, lots of them," Dr. Barnes said as he opened his medical bag.

"We've our petticoats," Miss Trump replied. "What else does thee need?"

By the time Maureen got back with the water, Dr. Barnes' instruments were assembled. Torn strips of white cotton petticoat lay in a pile. There was a heavy, sweet smell in the room, and the injured man appeared to be asleep.

Miss Trump spoke to the other black man. "Job, we must keep Amos very quiet while the doctor works. Nora, thee will tend to the chloroform. Dr. Barnes, is everything ready?"

"You, girl." The doctor addressed Maureen. "There's going to be a lot of blood. You must soak it up quickly with those rags so I can see to work. You understand?"

Maureen felt lightheaded but she was able to answer faintly, "Aye."

Amos let out a long, agonizing moan, unlike anything Maureen had ever heard. Mrs. Duffy leaned over him, covering his face with the chloroform-soaked rag. Maureen heard the doctor's saw bite into bone, then grate back and forth. She mopped at the blood which spurted from the man's leg. Minutes seemed hours and she lost track of the time passing.

Finally the bleeding parts were tied off. Dr. Barnes sewed the flaps of skin together, covering the stump. Maureen noticed for the first time that the doctor's shirt was wet with perspiration.

Amos' face was a sickly gray. He no longer moaned, but stared straight ahead in a drugged stupor. The man named Job began singing to him very softly.

Maureen heard Job's words, "carry you to freedom" and closed her eyes. "Such an awful price to pay," she murmured. "God help him."

"I've done all I can," the doctor said as he wiped his instruments. "It's fortunate Amos is a strong man. But he'll need a long rest. Even then, I can't guarantee . . ."

"He will recover, Doctor," Mrs. Duffy said firmly. "I know he will."

She began gathering up the bloody rags. "We must clean all this. Maureen, get more water. We don't want any evidence around."

Dr. Barnes had put on his suit jacket, preparing to leave. "Mrs. Duffy? There's the matter of my fee."

"Of course." Mrs. Duffy went over to her basket and took out the seedy-cake.

Maureen turned her head away. How could anyone think of eating cake *now*?

Then she looked back at Mrs. Duffy. The woman was lifting off the top part of the cake. It was hollow inside, and filled with dollar bills. Maureen stared. Had she gone daft?

Mrs. Duffy counted out ten dollars and handed them to the doctor. "You agreed to give us laudanum for Amos."

"I will," the doctor said, pocketing his money. "Have

you decent lodgings for him? He'll not get well here."

"We do."

"Good. I am sorry for the poor fellow, you know." The doctor finished packing his instruments and turned to Miss Trump. "I place myself in jeopardy, coming here. If word got out that I'd helped you Quakers—"

"Dr. Barnes, we appreciate the risk thee took," Miss Trump interrupted. "I believe thee has been well paid."

"Well, I must be on my way now." The doctor seemed uncomfortable. He gave Miss Trump a bottle of laudanum and hurried out the door.

"Mick should have been here by now," Mrs. Duffy said to Miss Trump. "Pray God he's not met any trouble."

Mick? Mick Duffy is involved in this, too? Maureen wondered.

In a few minutes there was a quiet tap at the door. Mrs. Duffy opened it and there stood her husband. He spotted Maureen and gave his wife an angry look.

"What's she doing here?"

"Maureen helped me carry the things from Oliver Street. When I saw what had happened to Amos, I called her in to help us. Mick, she can be trusted."

Maureen looked at Mr. Duffy and tried to think of what to say. "I, I wish these men no harm," she stammered.

"But there are others who do," he said sharply. He shook a finger at Maureen. "No one is to know what happened here today!"

Miss Trump was watching Amos with concern. "Did thee find a hiding place, Mick?" she asked.

"I did. The mews behind Charles Sinclair's. He's with us, and so is his cook. These two will be safe and well tended there."

"Thank the good Lord."

Amos and Job were carefully hidden under the straw in

Mick Duffy's wagon. After they departed Miss Trump spoke to Maureen. "Thee was very brave and of great help to us. But remember, mention these events to no one, not even thy closest friend. Other ears might hear, and there are people who would report Amos and Job for a pocket of reward money."

"I'll remember."

"God be with thee." Miss Trump put her arms around Mrs. Duffy. "Nora, we will meet at Circle on Wednesday?"

"Aye, Letty. Good night. God bless."

Maureen and Mrs. Duffy continued on along Monroe Street. The moon was full and bathed the streets in milky light. All was quiet, save the crickets singing to one another.

"Say what you're thinking, girl." Mrs. Duffy broke the silence.

"Oh, there's so much. Those two black men, they're slaves? Miss Trump said their master was after them. But how did they get to New York, especially Amos, with his leg torn?"

"Have you ever heard talk of an 'underground railroad'?"

"No."

"It's not really a railroad. It's many different paths, all of them going south to north, from slave state to free. Along those paths are stations, but only a few people know where they are. Could be a farmhouse, or a store, maybe a church.

"Now Letty Trump, and other folks, not just Quakers, they help a runaway slave get from station to station until he's safe. It's risky business. You see, someone in Maryland knew where Amos and Job were hiding, and told their master when he rode into town. Amos hurt his leg trying to escape."

"Aren't they safe in New York?"

The lines in Mrs. Duffy's face deepened. "Used to be, but no more. If a slave is found out, he can be sent right back to his master. Just like a horse that's run away."

"Then where will they go?"

"First off, we'll keep Amos well hidden till he's able to travel. Then it's further north, to Canada. He'll be safe there. And one day, slavery will come to an end."

"How?"

"Deep down inside, every man and woman in this country knows that slavery's wrong. More and more people will start saying it must be ended. You'll see." Mrs. Duffy took Maureen's hand. "Now don't go troubling yourself overmuch about what happened today. We all must travel the hard road sometime. But it takes us to a better place, surely."

Maureen nodded. They were nearly home and there was one thing she wanted to say before parting. "Mrs. Duffy? I'm glad you asked me to help with Amos, that you trusted me."

Mrs. Duffy smiled. "Aye, girl. Good night, now."

14
An Irish Washerwoman

Maureen stood in front of the large iron gate that guarded the entrance to the Winston Cabot residence. It was not yet eight o'clock in the morning.

Mrs. Duffy had sent Maureen to the Cabots' to see about the job as washerwoman.

"The housekeeper is the sister of Letty Trump, the Quaker woman at the warehouse," Mrs. Duffy had told Maureen, "and though she may be a stiff-nose, a fair-minded woman she is too. Hear me now, you go see her. The Cabots' is just uptown, across Seventh Avenue at Waverly Terrace."

Now that Maureen was here, her mouth went dry and she was tormented by nervous butterflies. She moved on tiptoe up the graceful walkway and around to the side of the mansion. At the servant's entrance she gave the knocker a rap and a young woman in a maid's uniform opened the door.

"Good morning. Is Miss Trump in, please?"

"She is." The maid paused. "But she's busy just now. What do you want?"

"I'm seeing about the job as washerwoman."

A sly smile crossed the maid's face and she turned to whisper a remark to someone. "You'll have to wait," she told Maureen.

Maureen could see into the large kitchen. Another woman, dressed in the same black and white uniform, held a tea tray. Behind her an older man sat at a table eating, and off in a corner, a young girl was chopping vegetables.

"Well, don't just stand and stare," the first maid snipped. "Are you coming in or not?" She pointed to a bench next to the door. "Wait there."

"Who's this, Cora?" The second maid was eyeing Maureen's shabby brogans. "Something just off the boat?"

"Why, Lizzie, the Papist fancies Beulah's job. She could use some scrubbing herself," Cora laughed.

Maureen's cheeks burned but she pretended not to hear the remarks.

The man at the table pushed back his chair and offered some bacon to a large tawny cat. "Here you are, Muffin. Eat up, now," he said.

The smell of bacon lingered in the air and Maureen found it nearly unbearable as she watched the cat eating.

The man appeared to be a gardener and took little notice of the two maids or Maureen as he went out the door. The scullery girl stayed in her corner, occasionally casting shy looks in Maureen's direction.

Cora and Lizzie moved to the pantry room off the kitchen where they whispered loudly to each other. Maureen heard Cora's voice, and the words "dirty Irish."

"A stick in your eye!" Maureen hissed under her breath.

The hallway door opened and a tall, dour-faced woman came in. She bore only the faintest resemblance to Letty Trump. The two maids came to attention.

"Good morning, Miss Trump. There's a girl to see you

about Beulah's job," Lizzie announced.

"An *Irish* girl," Cora added.

"Oh?" Miss Trump looked down her long nose at Maureen.

"Good morning to you, ma'am," Maureen said, rising from the bench. "It's Nora Duffy sent me, saying I should speak to you about the job as washerwoman. It's ever so hard-working I am, and most reliable. I won't be sick a day and will do as good a job as anyone you'd hope to find." The words came out in a long rushing stream.

Miss Trump regarded her coolly. "Would you repeat yourself, girl, and kindly do not run each word together or I will never understand you."

"It's Nora Duffy that sent me," she began again, "about a job as washerwoman. 'Twas said you wanted someone to do a decent day's work." Maureen's voice dropped to a whisper. " 'Twas said, too, you were fair-minded."

Miss Trump patted her nose with a handkerchief and turned to Cora and Lizzie. "You may go about your duties. Remember that Mrs. Cabot is not to be disturbed this morning."

"Yes, Miss Trump," the two answered in unison. Cora's eyes flicked to Maureen. "There's no place for you here," they seemed to say.

Miss Trump sat down at the kitchen table. "What is your name?"

"Maureen O'Connor."

"You must understand, Maureen, that the job of washerwoman is not a light one. Mrs. Cabot is very particular."

"Aye."

"We say 'yes,' not 'aye,' in this household. Now, the washerwoman must start the day early. There will be no coming in at half-ten with your skirts undone."

"Oh, I'll be here as early as you want, Miss Trump."

"And we do not allow foul language. Nor drinking and gambling of any sort."

"Oh, no, ma'am. None of that."

"There's the matter of your religion."

"Beg pardon?"

"You are Irish, and a Catholic, are you not?"

"Aye—I mean, yes, I am."

"Nora Duffy knows I do not judge people by their religions or origins. However," Miss Trump raised a hand to indicate the entire kitchen, "the other servants often object to Irish help."

Maureen knew what was coming next, but at least Miss Trump was being polite. Still, the results would be the same as at the match factory: another walk home, and no work.

Miss Trump stood up. "You may begin today. Your wages will be one dollar and fifty cents the week, paid on Saturday. Dinner is included each day. Come in at half-seven every morning but Sunday. Cook or Millie, the scullery maid, will let you in."

Maureen looked up blankly. Her ears were surely playing tricks on her.

"Come along, girl, the laundry is this way. Hurry now, the morning is getting on."

"Aye—yes, ma'am."

Maureen followed the housekeeper down into the dark cellar. Miss Trump lit a lamp and mounds of laundry emerged from the shadows. Nearby was a pump, and a small stove for heating water. At the far end of the cellar wooden steps led to an outside yard. Maureen glimpsed rows of clotheslines through the half-open door. There were lines in the cellar as well.

Miss Trump showed her the tins of matches, soap,

bluing and starch. "Servants' dinner is at two o'clock. Have you questions?"

Maureen shook her head, still uncertain that the job was truly hers.

"Good." The housekeeper turned and went upstairs.

For a moment Maureen stood looking around the cellar. Imagine, she was a washerwoman in a fine mansion. What news to take back to Oliver Street!

The morning flew. She heated water and plunged bared arms deep into the steaming washtub. The lye fumes stung her eyes and her hands hurt from the constant rubbing. Baskets of linens were hauled up the wooden steps and out to the clothesline. Slowly the piles of laundry diminished.

A loud knock came from the top of the cellar stairs. "You, girl, come and eat," someone called.

Maureen wiped her hands and tied back her damp hair. Water soaked her skirt and she shook it out as best she could. "A washerwoman I am, indeed."

Going up the stairs, she could smell freshly baked bread and a ravenous hunger overtook her. She came into the kitchen and nearly fainted at the sight of the meat, soup, bread, jugs of milk and barley water.

The cook was at one end of the table, the timid young kitchen maid sat on her left, and the gardener on her right. Miss Trump was seated at the opposite end, with the maids Cora and Lizzie on either side. There was no other place at the table.

"A plate for you is in the pantry, Maureen. You will eat there," Miss Trump said quietly. "As you can see, we have no room here."

A muffled snicker came from Cora.

"Oh." Maureen turned away from the table. She crossed the kitchen to the pantry, keenly aware of the eyes that followed her. "Not good enough for them, eh?" she fumed silently. "We'll see, one day."

Inside the pantry, Maureen closed the door. She stood there, eyes smarting. "No matter," she said, and made a face in the direction of the kitchen.

The pantry was a small room, filled with jars of food, crocks of vinegar and honey, tins of tea, coffee, flour. A kitchen stool was at one end, and on it Maureen saw a cloth-covered plate. Despite her hurt feelings, her mouth began to water. She lifted the napkin.

Nicely browned pieces of beef swam in a rich gravy. New potatoes nestled beside the meat next to buttered green beans, carrots, and two thick slices of currant bread. Atop the beef, its tiny paws curled inward, lay a dead mouse.

Maureen froze. Somehow she kept from crying out. Slowly getting up from the stool, she put the plate down and backed away. Her eyes were fixed on the mouse's gray coat, matted now from the gravy.

Maureen covered her mouth with her hands. She would not let Cora, or any of them, make her cry. She gritted her teeth and pictured herself dumping the plate of food all over the maid. "I'll get even with her! She can't be rid of me so easy."

Maureen lay the napkin on the floor and lifted the mouse onto it, folding the napkin securely. "I think I know of a nice place for you," she said, putting the mouse in the pocket of her skirt.

There was no use trying to eat the food on her plate. Maureen took a roll of butcher paper from the top shelf and wrapped the food into a small bundle. Going to the pantry window, she dropped the bundle outside.

She crept to the door and listened. Miss Trump and Cook were discussing Cook's visit to the doctor. Maureen waited a few minutes, then decided it was a good time to

85

return to the cellar. She opened the door.

"Cook, ma'am?" she said politely. "Thank you for a fine dinner. Where shall I put my plate?"

"Eh? Oh, there by the basin. Millie will see to it."

Maureen moved around the table. She stole a glance at Cora, who was staring at her in disbelief. Nodding to Miss Trump, she went back downstairs. She hid the mouse in the corner and resumed her laundry chores.

The afternoon seemed endless. Her complaining stomach reminded her that she had had nothing to eat since last night's tea and bread. The baskets of clothes grew heavier, the cellar steps became more difficult to climb.

Late in the day, her arms ached as she folded the dry linens. It would be a comfort to be back in the little room on Oliver Street. First, however, she must deal with the matter of the mouse, which still lay neatly wrapped in the napkin.

Miss Trump came down to inspect the day's work. "More scrubbing next time, Maureen," the housekeeper said, examining a shirt. "You may go now. And don't forget: half-seven tomorrow morning."

"Yes, ma'am. I'll be here."

The kitchen was deserted except for Millie. The scullery maid was off in the far corner of the room, scrubbing the floor. Two neatly ironed aprons hanging on the wall invited Maureen's attention. The longer one would surely be Cora's, for she was much taller than Lizzie.

Maureen loosened the napkin around the dead mouse. Quickly she stepped over to Cora's apron and slipped the mouse inside the pocket, pulling the napkin away at the same time. Ah, perfect!

"Good day, Millie," Maureen called cheerfully. "I'll see you in the morning."

The gardener was outside the potting shed smoking his pipe. "Good," thought Maureen. "Not likely he'll notice me at the pantry window." There, under a peony bush, was her dinner inside the roll of butcher paper.

Maureen picked up the package and tucked it under her arm. "Old Sal's dog, Barney, will have himself a nice meal tonight," she said.

15
A Familiar Face

Fall brought a crispness to the air. Maureen shivered and pulled her shawl snugly around her shoulders. Each day the colors in the trees along Waverly Terrace were more beautiful, and this morning the wind chased the leaves into golden whirlwinds about her feet.

It was Saturday, the end of her fourth week as washerwoman to the Cabots, and the day wages were paid. One dollar and fifty cents. Thinking of the money made the ache in her back less annoying.

Most of her pay would again go to Mr. Pike and Mrs. Maguire, the merchants to whom she owed money. Rent was still due Mrs. Duffy, although having Mr. O'Leary sharing the room had helped. A letter from Da had finally arrived last week, but no money came with it. There'd been a disagreement over his wages he said; next month he'd send something for sure.

With the weather turning cooler, Maureen planned to buy yarn for knitting caps and scarves. She worried about Brian and Paddy needing shoes. Although her own tattered brogans were a sorry sight, the boys had no shoes at all and, come winter, their feet would suffer.

Work at the Cabots' was going rather well. Maureen avoided Cora as much as possible and refused to let the maid's haughty manner bother her. The rest of the staff had become friendlier, although Millie seemed to think Maureen was going to put some evil Irish curse on her. "Silly thing," Maureen laughed to herself. "If only I had such power, sure wouldn't I use it?"

This morning the kitchen door opened before Maureen could knock. Cora glowered at her. "Well, about time! You picked a fine day to be late."

Maureen ignored the remark and stepped into the kitchen. Millie was standing in the corner, wringing her hands. The gardener sat scowling at his cup of tea. Lizzie and Miss Trump could be heard down the hall, talking in agitated voices. Cook was nowhere to be seen.

" 'Tis a bad humor everyone seems in today," Maureen thought as she opened the door to the cellar. "I'm well off having the laundry to myself."

But before Maureen could head down the stairs, Miss Trump called out to her from the hallway.

"Maureen, the washing will have to wait. Cook has been taken to the infirmary and you and Cora must help with the marketing."

Cora was tying on her bonnet and made a face as Miss Trump came into the kitchen.

"I'll not be seen with *her,* Miss Trump," she snapped.

"Mind your tongue," Miss Trump spoke sharply and handed the maid a market basket. "Here's your list; see that you pick the freshest goods."

Cora adjusted her bonnet and looked over her shoulder. "Tsk, tsk. The way some people dress." She tossed the remark at Maureen and flounced out the door.

"I want you to go to the butcher, Maureen. Mr. McPhee is a trustworthy gentleman. Tell him you're there for the Cabots; he'll give you his best cuts." Miss Trump held out a wicker basket and a small purse. "Go only to the butcher. No side trips or dallying, you understand?"

"Yes, ma'am."

Miss Trump gave Maureen directions to the shops. "I'll expect you back before long," she added.

Maureen put on her shawl and went out the door. How pleasant it was to be out-of-doors on such a glorious day instead of down in that damp old cellar.

She had no trouble finding the market area. It was busy with shoppers and the vendors were lustily trying to outshout one another. Maureen was reminded of the stalls near Oliver Street, except here the women were well dressed. She admired their bonnets and attractive woolen capes. Cora was nearby, leaning over a bin of onions. "Best I move on," Maureen murmured, "before Miss Nose-in-the-air sees me."

A large sign hung over the entrance to Mr. McPhee's butcher shop. "WE HAVE MEAT THAT'S FIT TO EAT" it read. A thick layer of sawdust covered the floor and at the back of the shop hung shanks of pork, lamb shoulders, sides of beef. The butcher took orders from behind a long wooden counter, cutting and weighing and engaging in lively gossip with his customers.

Maureen found Mr. McPhee's story of the Hamilton's parlor maid running off with their coachman quite enter-taining. Now she knew where Cook got all her news about the happenings in the neighborhood.

"Good mornin', lass. Are you interested in pork loin today? I've got the verra best, and at a good price for your mistress." The burr of his native Scotland rolled across Mr. McPhee's tongue.

"Oh, I'm here for the Cabots. Our cook's taken sick."

"Now I'm verra sorry to hear that. You tell her George McPhee sends his regards. What was it she wanted today?"

90

"Miss Trump wrote it down." Maureen handed the meat order to the butcher.

"All right, pork chops I've got, and a good roast of beef, too."

Mr. McPhee hummed as he weighed the meat and wrapped it. "There you are, lass. Seventy-five cents, please."

Maureen carefully counted out the money and put the packages into her basket.

"You tell Miss Trump, George said 'Hello.' "

"Aye then, I will. Good day to you, Mr. McPhee."

"Now if you'd asked for lemons, I'd have recognized you straight away."

These words came from behind Maureen. She blinked, thinking she had imagined them. That voice?

She turned slowly. He was just as she remembered him. His clothes were different, but the windburned face and the gray, seafaring eyes were surely the same. It was the young sailor from the *Western Star*.

"You?" she whispered. "Here?"

He smiled slightly and nodded. "Gave up sea life for a spell. And you, miss? You've settled in New York?"

"Edward? Is this a friend of yours?" A young woman with the sailor nodded questioningly at Maureen.

Maureen looked at her. She was pretty, with a flowered bonnet and lavender shawl that flattered her fair coloring. Maureen noted how the woman's hand was cozily tucked into the sailor's arm.

She felt confused and uncomfortably warm. Suddenly the butcher shop seemed very crowded.

"I—I must get back," Maureen said. "Miss Trump will be wondering . . ." She looked at the sailor and shook her head. "It's so strange, seeing you here. I never thought . . ." The words trailed off and she quickly made her way out to the street.

The sailor put down his toolbox and followed Maureen to the door. "But, miss, wait a moment—" Before he could say anything more, Maureen was lost in the crowd of shoppers.

Miss Trump was surprised and pleased at Maureen's prompt return. She unwrapped the meat, nodded her approval, and handed it to Millie.

"Mr. McPhee sends you his greetings," Maureen said.

Miss Trump smiled. "Well. A busy crowd there, I suppose?"

"Yes, ma'am," Maureen's heart still pounded from the run back to Waverly Terrace. "Shall I do the laundry now, Miss Trump?"

"Yes, very good, Maureen. And if Millie stops her sniveling, perhaps some order can be brought to this kitchen." The housekeeper gave a weary sigh.

Maureen went down to the cellar, glad for a place to collect her thoughts. She sat on the bottom step, staring at the piles of laundry.

Of all days for Cook to be sick, and of all the shops in New York City, today she was sent to Mr. McPhee's. And who should be there? The sailor from the *Western Star*. It was not something she'd dreamed. She had seen him, heard his voice. But why wasn't he at sea?

She chewed on the end of her thumb. The pretty young woman in the bonnet had called him "Edward." Maureen said the name aloud: "Edward." She shook her head. That woman . . . she must be his sweetheart and he has quit the *Star* to be with her. Aye, that must be it.

"Oh, what does it matter?" Maureen stood up and kicked at the pile of linens. "Do you expect these clothes to wash themselves?" she scolded. "Get on with your work, girl!"

92

16
Back to Oliver Street

By late afternoon the sky had darkened. A roll of thunder shook the house. Maureen thought of the long walk back to Oliver Street. Her wages were in her pocket and she held up a five-cent piece, debating whether to spend it for a ride on the omnibus.

She looked down at her brogans, at the holes where her leggings showed through, and thought of her brothers' bare feet. It would take a good deal of money to buy them shoes, and five cents was five cents. Besides, what was a little dampness? She would walk.

Outside, the wind whistled through the trees and sent the rain against her face. Maureen clutched her shawl and ran.

As she hurried along Waverly Terrace, footsteps sounded not far behind her. The rain fell more heavily and she quickened her pace.

Whoever was behind her began to move faster, too. All at once Maureen thought of the money in her pocket. Someone was after her wages! She held onto her shawl and ran as fast as she could.

"You, girl, wait up!" a voice called.

She kept running, glad for her long legs. Then some-thing occurred to her: she knew that voice. The same disbelief she had felt in the butcher shop came over her again. It couldn't be, yet it was.

She looked over her shoulder. The rain blurred the approaching figure, but soon the sailor caught up with her and took her arm.

"You've a good stride, girl," he said, panting. "You nearly got away again."

He was wearing his sailor's oils and the water ran off him in rivulets. Quickly he unhooked the oilcloth, slipping his arms out and extending part of the slicker across Maureen. Pointing to a nearby archway, he moved Maureen toward it.

For a moment neither of them spoke. Maureen made little puffs of steam as she caught her breath. She could feel the warmth of the sailor close to her beneath the slicker.

"Perhaps I'm daft," she said, "for twice today I've seen a sailor I thought was at sea."

He smiled. "I feel a bit daft myself. I . . . I don't even know your name."

Maureen paused. " 'Tis Maureen O'Connor." She looked up at him and thought of the young woman in the butcher shop.

"Maureen, is it? I wondered." The sailor straightened and gave a mock salute. "Edward Cooke, ma'am. A former purveyor of lemons, and now a landlocked carpenter."

"Then . . . you've left the sea?"

Edward's expression sobered. "A sailor never quite does that; the salt air's in his blood. But . . . I wanted a look at America." He frowned. "What about your brother? The one who was sick?"

"Paddy. He got better after I gave him the lemons. I'm

certain they helped him. I . . . I'm sorry that I never properly thanked you for your kindness."

" 'Twas no need. I'm glad to hear he's well." Edward stared out at the rain and his gray eyes were thoughtful. " 'Twas a hard crossing, that one."

"Aye. At times I feared we'd never see land again."

"I'd not sailed with an immigrant ship before and only signed on the *Star* at the last minute." The sailor's voice grew quiet. "The *Star* was in trouble the day Hawkins came aboard her. Not only did he cheat the passengers, he was a bad mate as well."

The rain continued to drum against the cobblestones. The lamplighter was late making his rounds and the street was dark.

"This puts me in mind of that night in the galley," Maureen said. "Sure I never expected we'd meet again in the rain." She gave him a questioning look. "Edward? Do you live nearby?"

He laughed shortly and slapped the sides of his trousers. "It's too fancy a neighborhood for these pockets. I was over visiting Miss Adams. Her father owns the dry dock where I'm working now. They live up a ways, near the square."

"Oh."

"If you're wondering how I came to be chasing after you in the rain, I asked the butcher where you worked."

Maureen looked down, aware of the high color in her cheeks. A breeze whiffled through the archway and she began to shiver.

"Are you cold, Maureen?"

"Aye . . . a bit."

"No wonder. You're soaking wet." Edward took a navy kerchief from his pocket.

"Oh, your kerchief," Maureen said with a start. "The

95

one you gave me on the *Star* . . . I still have it."

Edward raised his eyebrows. "Ah-ha. I knew I had cause to see you again." He gently wiped at the water trickling down the side of her face. "So it's Maureen? A pretty name. I'm thinking it suits you."

Maureen turned away, reluctant to let the sailor see how much his words had pleased her.

Quite suddenly the rain stopped.

The streets were quiet except for the sound of water rushing along the gutters. Somewhere a dog began to bark.

Edward stepped from the archway. "I'd say that's the end of it. Look, even Pegasus has come out. See there." He pointed to the constellation.

"Ah, the four stars?"

The sailor took his oilcloth and shook the water from it. He turned and looked at Maureen.

"It's getting cold. How far to where you live?

"Past Canal and down. Oliver Street."

"Gorblimy, that's three miles or more. You'll catch your death."

"I don't—" Maureen started.

"Listen, the omnibus is just one block away. I can see you home; it won't be any trouble. I bunk over at the dry dock."

He reached into his pocket. "Come on, I'll get your fare."

She followed him as he ran up the block, leaping across the puddles left by the storm. When they got to Bleecker Street he waved down the approaching omnibus.

"Two fares? Ten cents, please." The conductor looked at them. "A couple o' wet ducks, eh?" he said with a wink.

The omnibus was an enclosed wagon with two long benches, covered with a metal canopy and pulled by four

96

strapping dray horses. Across the canopy were the words "Canal Street."

There was only one empty seat on the bus. Maureen hesitated, then made her way over to it, and Edward came and stood next to her, bracing one hand against the canopy for support. At a call from the conductor, the horses moved forward.

People got on and off the omnibus as it traveled down Wooster to Canal and then headed east. Maureen was happy to be nestled between the other riders, away from the damp wind. She watched the passing buildings, surprised at how fast the bus was going.

Edward carefully eyed the street signs. "The conductor said we'll have to get off at the Bowery. He doesn't turn south."

Just then came the call, "The Bowery, next stop!"

"That's us."

The omnibus came to a halt. Edward hopped down and put his hand up to assist Maureen. He was looking at her with such seriousness she wondered if something was wrong.

"I've been thinking of the day the *Star* landed in New York," he said. "Do you know, I felt sure I was going to meet you again someday."

" 'Tis strange, indeed. Only because Cook took ill was I in the butcher's today, for I'm the Cabots' washerwoman and am seldom out of the cellar."

"Then I owe Cook my thanks," Edward said. "Otherwise, I'd still be wondering, 'What ever happened to that dark-haired Irish girl?' " He narrowed his eyes. "Ran off with my kerchief, she did."

The night air had a chill to it. They walked briskly, ducking the raindrops blown off the trees by the wind.

"You were with your father and brothers on the *Star?*"

asked Edward. "What of your mother?"

"She was too weak for a long journey. She's still in Ireland, with Uncle Owen. Pray God, she'll join us before long."

Maureen began to shiver again. "Come on, lass," said Edward, "we'd best hurry."

They ran down the Bowery and past Chatham Square, then slowed to a walk as they neared Oliver Street. Edward looked around the neighborhood. "I've never been down this far. Does your pa work nearby?"

"No. He had to go to the coal mines in Pennsylvania."

"Then it's only your brothers and yourself live here?"

"Aye. And Mr. O'Leary. He shares our room. Perhaps you could come up for a cup of tea? It will warm you a bit; and what a surprise for the boys, seeing you."

"Well . . ."

" 'Tis no trouble, Edward, for—" Maureen stopped in midsentence. Three boys were loitering on the corner, their collars turned up against the wind.

"Why, that's Paddy." Maureen pointed to the tallest of the trio.

As she and Edward neared the corner the boys glanced over at them. Maureen saw that her brother was puffing on a cigarette. "Hello, Paddy," she said, ignoring his smoking. "See who's here in New York!"

The boy took a step backwards. He seemed puzzled as he looked at Edward and then at Maureen. "Isn't he—?"

"That's right. 'Tis the sailor from the *Star*. He gave me the lemons when you were sick, remember?"

Paddy fumbled with his cigarette. "Oh, aye." He kept his head down and nudged his companions. "He's rotten English."

Paddy's friends stood with thumbs hooked in their pockets, eyeing the sailor. "We don't much like the

English down here," one of the boys said. "We's Irish."

"I see," Edward replied. He looked up the street. "But this isn't Ireland."

"Makes no difference," Paddy interjected.

Maureen was stunned. "Begging your pardon, Paddy O'Connor, but it does. You've no call to say such to Edward after what he did for you."

Paddy threw his cigarette into the gutter and turned to his friends. "We better get over to Whacker's. He wants help with those rally flyers tonight."

The three boys went off together, Paddy in the lead. Maureen stared at them, her eyes stinging. "I don't understand that boy," she said. "Sure I'm . . . I'm sorry, Edward, for what was said."

"Oh, no matter. I expect he fancies himself all grown-up."

"Humph. Well, Brian will be pleased to see you. And you can meet our boarder, as well. Mr. O'Leary's very nice."

"Ah, Maureen? Many thanks, but I should be moving on, for I go up to Tarrytown early tomorrow, to work on Mr. Adams' clipper. Perhaps another time we can have tea?"

"Oh . . . very well."

"I'll be gone for a few days. I was wondering . . . may I call on you when I return?"

Maureen brightened. "Aye, Edward. I mean—'yes', it would please me entirely to see you again."

They stood silently in front of the lodging house. Tim the Lamplighter was finishing his rounds and doffed his cap as he passed by.

"Thank you, Edward, for taking me home," said Maureen. "And please, pay no heed to what Paddy said."

"Ah, don't worry. A sailor hears much worse." Edward

took Maureen's hand and held it for a moment. "Stay out of the rain now, Miss O'Connor. Good night."

Mr. O'Leary and Brian were at the table studying one of Mr. O'Leary's maps. "The rain catch you, did it?" said Mr. O'Leary, looking up as Maureen came in the door.

She nodded. "I . . . I came home on the omnibus, so's not to get a chill."

Maureen went over to the table. "Brian, the strangest thing happened today. Miss Trump sent me off to the butcher's, and who do you think I saw there? Someone from the *Western Star!*"

Brian shrugged. "The Widow Fitzpatrick?"

"Oh my, no. 'Twas the young sailor, the one who gave me the lemons for Paddy."

"In a butcher shop? Sure that's an odd place for a sailor."

Maureen laughed. "He's quit the sea and works as a carpenter now, right here in New York."

The door opened and Paddy came in. He seemed in a hurry and went directly to the burlap bag where the family's belongings were kept. He began rummaging through the bag, an intent frown on his face.

"What are you looking for, may I ask?" Maureen said frostily, still feeling annoyed with him for his rudeness to Edward.

"Da's old cap," came the reply, equally cool. "Ah, here it is. I thought he'd left this one behind."

The boy held out a frayed cloth cap, cut low to the brim and showing years of wear. He put it on, pulling it down in the front so it nearly covered one eye. It was too big but he seemed not to care.

Maureen was watching him. "Aren't you the man?" she said, tossing her head. "And an ungrateful one too, I might add."

100

Paddy looked at her with that stubborn jut to his chin that she knew so well from Da.

"Really, Paddy, at least you could have been polite. Edward took a risk—"

"I have to go," Paddy interrupted. "Whacker's having a meeting tonight; he wants me there." With an air of importance he patted the cap and went to the door. "You don't have to wait up," he said, and was gone.

"Oh, bother Whacker Nolan!" Maureen shouted after him, then glanced sheepishly at Mr. O'Leary. "I'm sorry. But . . . Paddy's never home any more. He's always out with that Nolan gang. . . . a bunch of ruffians." She sat down and gave an unhappy sigh. "Things just haven't been the same since Da went away."

17
A Rally in Oak Park

Mr. O'Leary was finishing his dinner when Maureen and Brian returned from Sunday Mass at St. Brendan's. Maureen had to smile; every meal Mr. O'Leary prepared was the same: two boiled potatoes and a jar of buttermilk.

He saw her expression and shook his head. "I know 'twas the praties that failed us. But I've a great fondness for them still."

They both laughed.

"Did you hear about the rally down at the park this afternoon?" Brian asked Mr. O'Leary.

"The one for Brendan Dooley?"

"Aye. Do you know him?"

"Dooley ran the Work Exchange when I first arrived. Helped me get on at the knackers, in fact. 'Course, no one else wants work skinning horses."

"Mr. Dooley is a friend of Whacker's, Paddy says. He claims Mr. Dooley will be mayor someday."

"Well, Dooley is a smart man. There's many Irish come over these past few years; that's a power of votes and he's a flinty eye for such things." Mr. O'Leary smiled. "Go hear the fellow; you'll have your entertainment. Dooley's one for the stage, all right."

"Will you be going?"

"I've heard him before. Besides, a friend has promised me the lend of a fishing pole. We're off to the Battery to try for some big ones."

"Oh? Well, good luck then," said Maureen. "I expect Brian and I will give a listen at the rally. After Paddy's grand talk about this Dooley fellow, I'm rather curious."

Maureen fixed tea and boiled cabbage for Brian and herself. She wished her Sunday dinner was not such a dull offering. During the week she would frequently bring home leftovers from her meal at the Cabots'. Sometimes Mrs. Rothman gave Brian a few eggs or Mr. O'Leary would buy sausage rolls for a special treat. On Sundays, however, there was little else on the O'Connors' table except tea and boiled cabbage.

Brian did not complain, but the wistful look in his eye told Maureen he envied Paddy the meat pies and beer that Whacker Nolan made available for his gang.

Oak Park was crowded by the time Maureen and Brian arrived. Families arranged themselves near the speaker's platform, laying down blankets and picnic baskets. Children chased in and out of the bushes while young couples strolled arm-in-arm across the greensward.

Large posters with Brendan Dooley's likeness decorated the park. Signs reading "VOTE IRISH—VOTE DOOLEY" were everywhere. Maureen recognized Dooley in a group of men up on the stage. There, too, was Whacker Nolan. No doubt Paddy was nearby.

Someone in front of the stage waved and motioned for Maureen to come over.

"Brian, there's Mrs. Duffy. Why don't we join her?"

"I'd like to try and find Paddy."

"Oh, all right. Then I'll see you later?"

The area in front of the stage was thick with spectators and Maureen had to step carefully over blankets and sleeping babies in order to get to Mrs. Duffy. "Thank you for saving me a place," she said. " 'Tis more crowded than I thought it would be."

Just then a man came to the center of the stage and raised his arms. "Ladies and gentlemen, quiet please! May I have your attention? Today we have with us a true son of Ireland. A man like yourselves, who fled the oppression of the English, only to find more hardship here in America. But this man will fight for our rights!"

The crowd grew quiet. All eyes were on Dooley, who stood with shoulders thrown back, a resolute expression on his face.

"Here is a man who has dug ditches with you; whose interests are *your* interests. I give you our next alderman, Brendan Dooley!"

The crowd burst into warm applause.

Brendan Dooley spread his hands out in a gesture of humble gratitude. He waved and smiled at the crowd. When the noise died down, he began.

"Thank you, my friends. What pleasure it gives me to see all of you today."

His face grew somber. "Many of us came to America to begin our lives anew. And what do we find? 'NO IRISH NEED APPLY!' Except at the dump, or in gas-filled sewers, or down dark alleys where the rats fight us for food!" He paused, letting the words sink in while a murmur of agreement floated through the crowd.

"But here there are no English laws to deny us our vote. Elect me your alderman—I'll see that you have good jobs and decent housing; your children can—"

Not far from Maureen a small, earnest man in beard and eyeglasses spoke up. "See here, Mr. Dooley, you've a lot of grand words. But what if there aren't enough jobs? The Germans and the Scots, they want work, too. I say, get rid of the bosses, spread the wealth around. Then *everyone* will be treated fairly; not just the Irish."

Suddenly two boys began jostling the man while a third boy slipped behind him and kneeled down. Maureen realized that one of the boys was Paddy. He roughly pushed the man, causing him to fall back over the kneeling boy.

The man struggled to his feet, waving his broken glasses as the boys made a fast retreat through the crowd.

"Paddy," Maureen breathed, "for shame!"

"Please, my friends," Dooley shouted to regain the crowd's attention. "May I point out to you the Widow McGrath? Now, when Danny McGrath, God rest him, was killed by a coal wagon, his wife and children were put out on the street for lack of rent. So I went around to the shop owners and the pubs, and I said: 'Can you spare something for a widow and her children?' Friends, the generosity I witnessed brought tears to my eyes.

"And that money didn't go to buy Brendan Dooley a new suit. It went to put a roof over Kitty McGrath and a bowl of stirabout in front of her little ones."

The crowd applauded warmly. Maureen leaned over to Nora Duffy. "He is a good man."

Mrs. Duffy was clapping, but not with the crowd's enthusiasm. "My girl, a man on a soapbox makes lovely noises," she said. "But you must hear him at his own table to know the truth of his words."

Dooley continued talking about the upcoming election. Hecklers were shouted down and Dooley acknowledged the crowd's support with smiles and handshakes. It was late afternoon when the rally finally came to an end. Sleepy children tagged behind their parents as they left the park. Courting couples lingered in the gathering twilight.

"Oh my, I'm too old to sit on the ground so long," Mrs. Duffy said, rubbing her back.

Maureen was folding the blanket when she saw Brian coming toward her. "There you are," he said. "Mrs. Maguire is having a meeting back of the grocery tonight. She wants me to run beer growlers for her from Larkin's Pub."

"Very well. Just be sure she pays you for your efforts," Maureen cautioned. "And with money, not beer, understand?"

Maureen and Mrs. Duffy came to the path leading out to James Street. "I need to call on Annie O'Brien," Mrs. Duffy said. "Her baby has been sick. You'll not mind walking back alone?"

"Not at all. And thank you for sharing your blanket. I'm glad I came today."

As she turned to leave, Mrs. Duffy nudged Maureen. "Now don't be mooning over those couples with a wish in your eye. There's many a handsome Irish lad will be glad of your company soon enough."

Maureen reddened. She had been watching the young men and women, but it was not any Irish fellow that had come to mind. "There's no wish in my eye at all, Mrs. Duffy," she said firmly.

Mrs. Duffy made a scoffing sound and bid Maureen good night.

The sun was setting and Maureen hunched her shoulders against the cool evening air. "Soon it will be dark when I leave the Cabots' at the end of the day," she said to herself.

She thought about Paddy and the shoving incident during the rally. What troubled her most was the look on her brother's face. He had been serious; pushing the man down was no light-hearted prank. And the other boys, they had acted the same. What meanness had got into them?

By the time she reached Oliver Street it was nearly dark. She could see the outline of Tim the Lamplighter climbing his ladder at the end of the block. A moment later a small circle of yellow light flickered in the gloaming.

Maureen looked up at the O'Connors' window. No one else was home yet. Probably Mr. O'Leary had stopped by the pub with his friend.

The flat was cold and dark. Maureen felt her way to the stove, reaching for the matches to light the oil lamp. As she adjusted the wick an odd feeling came over her, as if she were not alone. Her fingers fumbled with the match and before she could coax the flame, the floor behind her gave a loud creak.

Maureen whirled about. The shadowy outline of a man could be seen standing in the corner, next to the door. The figure came towards her and for one awful moment she could neither move nor breathe. A cry rose in her throat as the man put his hand out to her.

"Maureen!"

She stared in disbelief. It was Da.

18
Trouble in the Mines

Da came forward and put his arms around Maureen. "Oh, daughter," he whispered, "I wondered would you still be here."

"Is it really you?" Maureen cried. His jacket was rough against her face.

In the yellow lamplight she could see how haggard he was. There were dark circles around his eyes and his clothes were torn in several places. One leg dragged as he moved to the table.

"Is . . . everything all right?" she asked.

"Would there be a cup of tea, Maureen? And something to eat?"

"Eat?" She remembered the cabbage that had been set aside for Paddy. "There's only this. But we've tea; I'll put the kettle on."

He shoveled the cabbage into his mouth while she made the tea. Maureen saw that his boots were caked with mud, and he was obviously exhausted. She began to feel more and more uneasy.

He smiled wearily when she set the tea in front of him. "How I've longed for a cup of tea," he said. "The comfort in such a simple thing."

She sat down at the table, noticing now the deep gash along his chin. Her uneasiness hardened into fear.

Da stiffened when he spotted Mr. O'Leary's belongings.

"Who else is here, Maureen? And where are the boys?"

"Mr. O'Leary shares the flat. He's very nice; he works down at the knackers. Brian and Paddy are . . . running errands."

Da got up and edged towards the window, standing to one side and peering out. "I . . . I shouldn't have come here. I don't want trouble for you and the boys, but I had to see you."

Maureen couldn't bear it anymore, not knowing what was wrong. "Da! What has happened? Please, tell me!"

He came back to the table. "That ladder at the end of the hall, it goes to the roof?"

"Aye."

"Come, better we talk up there. Then I must go."

He opened the door cautiously and crept down the hall. Maureen winced, seeing how the one leg hurt him as he walked.

It was cold and blustery up on the roof. They stood close together next to the chimney, shielding themselves from the wind. Clouds scudded across the sky, hiding the moon.

"Listen carefully, Maureen. There's much to tell, and little time.

"The mines . . . there was trouble from the start. We were like moles in those tunnels, on hands and knees the entire shift, our lungs black with dust. Then there was the blasting . . . a young fellow lost an arm to the dynamite our second day in.

"But a man will endure many things for a wad o' money. Kevin and I agreed, we'd stay in those pits. Then came payday."

Da laughed bitterly. "Oh, payday it was, for the mine

owner. We were docked for our lodgings, for food, for picks and hats. Aye, even for candles to light the tunnels. I hadn't a penny left over, to send you."

"It's all right, Da; we've managed," Maureen interrupted.

"It's *not* all right, daughter. The bosses meant to take whatever we earned."

"Is that why you came back? Did Kevin come with you?"

Da made a sucking noise through his teeth. "Kevin Mahoney, God rest him, is at the bottom of the Allentown Mine."

"What?"

"He's dead, Maureen. That fool pit boss ordered blasting in the tunnel next to Kevin's. There was a cave-in; the men hadn't a chance."

"No, Da."

"We all went out then, on strike. There were threats aplenty, and ugly talk. Men saying it was murder, what happened.

"Jimmy Fogarty lost his brother in the cave-in. That night he said he'd make the company pay for killing those men." Da's voice dropped to a whisper. "I offered to help him.

"Our plan was to blow up the biggest mine, the Number Four. Jimmy had the dynamite; I was to stand watch.

"It was a perfect job. Buried everything, pit cars and all.

"Then Jimmy said we'd enough sticks left to take the store, too. Finish off the company good. But Kingsley, the pit boss, tried to stop us. Jimmy laid him cold, then set the caps. When the place blew . . . Kingsley went up with it."

Maureen was stunned. Da was right next to her, yet his voice seemed that of a stranger. "But *you* didn't do it. . . ." she began.

"I helped Jimmy, Maureen. It's my doing as much as

110

his. And 'twas known I blamed Kingsley for Kevin's death."

"Oh, Da! What will happen?"

"The company sent Otto Krebbs and his men after us. They're good trackers; Jimmy was caught before we reached Roaring Creek. I hid out, but they're not far behind me, 'tis certain."

"Will they come here?"

"More than likely. If they do, you say your da's in Pennsylvania; you've not seen him. Don't believe anything they say, Maureen!"

"Where will you go?"

"I'm not sure, yet. Maybe out west, someplace far away, till this blows over."

"But what about Ma?"

Da gripped Maureen's shoulders. "I didn't mean for this to happen, daughter. I'll get Ma here somehow. Only everything keeps going wrong! I . . . I don't know anymore what to do."

Maureen fought back tears. It wasn't like Da, to talk this way. All at once she remembered the two black men in the warehouse. They had been hunted and had found means of escape. "Da! Mrs. Duffy might know of a way . . . perhaps, perhaps she can help you!"

"No, Maureen. You mustn't tell anyone I'm here!"

"But she'll understand, I know she will. Let me go talk to her." Maureen moved away from the chimney, toward the trapdoor.

"Wait, it's too risky."

"Da, please trust me. I won't be long." She disappeared down the ladder.

Mrs. Duffy answered Maureen's urgent knock. "Why, I thought it was Mick," she said, "More than once that man has gone off without his key."

"Could I talk to you, Mrs. Duffy? 'Tis important."

"I expect I've no choice," Mrs. Duffy remarked as Maureen hurried in the door. "You're white as a sheet, girl. Sure nothing ails you?"

" 'Tis my da! There's been trouble in the mines, and . . ." Maureen paused, wondering how much to tell. "I'm asking if, if the Underground Railroad would help him, like it did for those slaves?"

Mrs. Duffy looked at her sharply. "Now slow your tongue. What do you mean, 'trouble'? Where is your da?"

"I . . .he . . ." Maureen's eyes turned toward the ceiling.

"Tell me what has happened, Maureen. Not a word will go beyond this room, if that's your wish."

Maureen bit her lip. She *had* to trust Mrs. Duffy. "Kevin Mahoney and some other men were killed when a mine caved in."

Mrs. Duffy looked down. "*Och,* God keep them," she murmured while crossing herself.

"Now Da's in trouble, for trying to get back at the men who caused the cave-in. One of them . . . was killed. Da didn't mean for such to happen, Mrs. Duffy! Don't you see, he has to get away."

Mrs. Duffy sat quietly in her chair, fingering the chipped edge of her teacup. Maureen glanced anxiously toward the door.

"I don't know what to tell you, Maureen. We're having enough trouble in the Underground now, without detectives and the like sniffing around."

"But couldn't you—?"

Mrs. Duffy shook her head. "There's risks aplenty. Besides, 'tis not only for me to decide." She reached out and touched Maureen's hand. "But I'll see what I can do. No promises, mind. Come back tomorrow evening, after I've spoken with Letty Trump. Meanwhile, keep your da well hidden, and not a word of this to anyone."

Maureen's eyes filled with tears. "Sorry I am to burden you, Mrs. Duffy, only . . . 'tis my da."

"I know, girl. Run along, now."

Maureen flew up the stairs. As she reached the landing she could hear Mr. O'Leary in the room, humming to himself. She tiptoed past the door and down to the end of the hall.

A rush of cold air met her as she pushed open the trapdoor to the roof. "Da?" she called softly.

He was no longer standing beside the chimney. She looked around. The wind rustled the mint and in the darkness the long wooden boxes resembled black coffins.

"Da?" she called again. Still no answer. She peered into the shadows of the neighboring rooftops. There was no sign of him anywhere.

19
Two Visitors

Mr. O'Leary looked up and smiled as Maureen came in. "Good evening, lass."

"Good evening, Mr. O'Leary." She tried to appear unconcerned. "Ah . . . how was the fishing?"

"Oh me, don't ask. Between Pat and myself, I think we fed worms to every fish in the harbor. And not a one 'twas grateful enough to stay on my line."

Maureen glanced around the room. "The boys aren't back yet?"

"No one was here when I came in. But the lamp was burning."

"I . . I was down at the privy."

Mr. O'Leary had a stack of bills and coins laid out on the table. He finished counting and slapped his leg triumphantly. "Well done! Another month and I'll be able to send for Bridget and the children. Come spring, it's good-by knackers, hello Missouri."

"Missouri?"

"St. Louis. There's opportunity out there, what with the railroads booming and all. More room, too. I'm thinking 'tis a better place for us than New York."

Aye, thought Maureen. A better place for Da, as well.

Mr. O'Leary collected his money and wrapped it tightly in an old stocking. "Another thing," he said, holding out his jacket, "these work clothes go into the fire the day Bridget comes off that boat. The very smell of them would knock her into next week."

There was a sound outside the door and Maureen jumped.

"Aren't you the jackrabbit tonight?" Mr. O'Leary chuckled.

Brian came in the door, looking very tired.

"Good evening, lad."

The boy grunted and sat down on the bed. "It's a wonder these legs o' mine aren't worn away to stumps. Every shopkeeper in the neighborhood was in Maguire's tonight. A thirsty crowd, too, and only me running the beer back and forth from Larkin's. There was a lot of talk about that fellow Dooley."

"Did you see Paddy at all?" asked Maureen, recalling the shoving incident at the rally.

"I did." Brian propped his chin in his hands and stared glumly at the wall. "Whacker had a big kegger going out behind Larkin's. Beer and eats aplenty. But just for his gang."

There was a scuffling noise on the stairs. Could it be Da, Maureen wondered, her eyes riveted on the door. More scuffling could be heard, and then a bumping sound. The door opened and two boys, a third slung between them, stood there.

"Evening, ma'am," one of the boys said groggily. "Paddy live here, does he?"

Maureen ran over to Paddy, who was suspended between the two other boys. His shirt had a long rip down the front and a good-sized bruise darkened his forehead. All three boys reeked of stale beer.

Maureen drew in her breath. "Jesus, Mary and Joseph!"

"No, ma'am, we's Arthur, Paddy and Desmond."

Maureen clenched her fists. "Would you mind telling me what has happened?"

"Nothin'. Jes' a fren'ly fight, s'all. We's bringin' him home to show we's still fren's."

The two boys untangled Paddy and he slipped to the floor. Maureen grabbed hold of him. "Brian, help me get this lump into bed," she called.

The boy was dragged across the room. "You picked a fine time to come home drunk," she scolded. She was about to mention Da and then caught herself. Turning angrily to Paddy's companions, she hissed: "Shove off before I take a stick to you." The boys went clattering down the stairs.

The Cabots' kitchen was in a terrible state when Maureen arrived the next morning. Cook's illness had worsened and she'd been sent to the country for a week's rest. Millie had managed to fumble even the simplest tasks, leaving burned bacon, scorched pans and soggy biscuits in her wake. To everyone's relief, Miss Trump announced that a replacement cook would arrive that day.

The new cook's name was Hagen. Not Miss, or Mrs., but just "Hagen." She was stout, with bristly hairs on her chin and false teeth that made a clicking noise when she talked. She immediately began getting the kitchen in order and soon had a market list prepared. Maureen was called up from the cellar.

"Miss Trump says you're to help with the marketing," Hagen said.

"Yes, ma'am?"

"I want potatoes, but not yer ordinary spuds. It's Carolinas I mean. They're sweet, and a golden color. Be sure you get the right ones, now."

"Carolinas?" Maureen frowned as she took the shopping basket. She had never heard of potatoes that were sweet.

When she reached the market she wandered among the stalls looking for the potatoes the new cook had described. "Oh, dear," she murmured. "I wonder will Hagen be very angry if I can't find them?"

She was about to give up when a huckster down the row called out: "Carolinas here, just up from the South! Carolina sweets, fine and good!"

"Ah," Maureen said, hurrying down to the man's cart. But instead of potatoes, she found a pile of oblong, golden tubers.

"Yes, miss, can I help you?" The vendor held up one of the potatoes. "Sweetest Carolinas in all New York. Arrived today, they did."

Maureen looked doubtful. "I'll take three pounds of those," she said, pointing to the sweet potatoes. As the vendor weighed them Maureen noticed a crowd had gathered a short distance away. There appeared to be a disturbance around one of the large produce wagons. She craned her neck, trying to see what was happening.

The vendor jerked his head in the direction of the crowd. "Hooper found a darky hiding in the wagon when he unloaded. Runaway slave. The men figure he rode all the way from Raleigh under these Carolinas."

Maureen paled. She stared at the crowd. "What are they going to do?"

"Oh, turn him in, I'll wager. Hooper says the reward should be his, seeing as how he caught the runaway. But Morris thinks since it's his wagon, he ought to get some of the money, too."

The vendor frowned as he put the potatoes in Maureen's basket. "I don't know," he said. "A fellow gets this far, why not let him go free?"

Maureen nodded and paid the man. She stood by

the cart, watching the crowd. The memory of Job and Amos and the worry over Da brought a sickening feeling to her stomach. Da had never come back last night.

"You all right, miss?" the vendor asked.

Maureen did not answer, but turned and slowly walked away.

"Very nice," Hagen said when Maureen returned to the Cabots'. She clicked her teeth as she examined the potatoes. "These are lovely."

Maureen sat through dinner unable to eat. Even when a dessert of warm apple pudding was brought to the table, she had no interest in food. She kept remembering how hungry Da had been yesterday and the way he'd stuffed the chunks of cold cabbage into his mouth.

Miss Trump looked at her. "Maureen, you're very wan today."

"I . . ."

"You're not well; I can see that. When you've finished the linens and the master's shirts, you may go on home. But mind you don't forget the starch."

Maureen thanked Miss Trump and returned to the cellar. She quickly attended to the linens and began mixing starch and water together for Mr. Cabot's shirts. "I'll be home before dark and can look for Da again. Pray God he's on the roof, or nearby," she said aloud.

There was a nip in the air and Maureen hugged her shawl tightly as she left the Cabots'. She shivered. Each day it seemed that winter was edging closer and closer to New York.

"Hello." Someone came from behind the Cabots' gatepost.

"Edward!" Maureen's mouth opened in surprise.

"I didn't go to Tarrytown after all. Mr. Adams wants us

to finish his cabinets first." He paused. "I thought we might walk a ways together."

"Oh."

"Or are you taking the omnibus?"

"No . . ."

He began walking beside her. She glanced at him and felt the pleasant nervous flutter she'd noticed that day in the rain. Only now the sensation combined with her thoughts about Da, making an awful knot in her stomach.

"In a hurry, are you?"

"Aye, a bit." She tried to smile. "I've . . . promised to help a neighbor tonight. She's . . . feeling poorly."

They continued walking together, neither of them saying anything. Edward whistled a little tune and when Maureen looked at him he smiled in a serious sort of way.

She wondered if he planned to go as far as Oliver Street with her. She was pleased to see him, but uneasy, too. There was so much to be reckoned with just now.

It was dusk by the time they reached Chatham Square. A line of children playing crack-the-whip came charging across the green. Edward took Maureen's hand as the squealing children ran past them.

"Well," he said. "You're nearly home. I'll go down Park Row; get me back to the dry dock before Nels lets the beans boil over again." Edward shifted his weight to his other foot and cleared his throat. "Listen, Maureen . . . I wondered if you'd be free on Sunday? We could go down to the Battery, to the park there."

Maureen felt her heart leap. "I . . . I can't be certain, if I'll be free."

"What if I stop by Oliver Street on Sunday? Say, half-eleven? If you can't come along, I'll try my luck another day." He gave her hand a squeeze.

"Edward, I hope I can go. Truly."

"I hope so, as well. Good night." He let go of her hand.

"Good night," she called as he went across the square. Her hand was warm from his holding it. "Sunday," she said, " . . . if all goes well."

Three more blocks to Oliver Street. As she neared the lodging house she worried that each passing stranger might be a detective. Or an informer. What if Da had been caught?

Mrs. Duffy's flat was in darkness. She must not be home yet, thought Maureen. But a light was in the O'Connors' window.

Brian was seated at the table, two books and a writing pad in front of him.

"Hi, Maureen," he greeted her.

Maureen looked carefully around the flat. "No one else here?"

"Just me."

"You haven't seen Mrs. Duffy?"

"Nope."

"Well." She looked around the room again, aware that Brian was watching her.

"Oh, don't mind me," she said. "It's a decent cup of tea I'm needing. Have we bread?"

"A two-penny rye. It was all that was left on the wagon this morning."

Maureen dipped water from the jug into the kettle. She kindled the stove wood and went to stand at the window while the water heated. Perhaps Da was waiting for her on the roof. She'd sneak up there soon, and have a look.

Brian was working at his tablet, writing with great endeavor. His industry caught Maureen's attention and she came to look over his shoulder.

"You mean *you* did all that?" she asked him.

The boy finished a line and held the pad out to her. "Aye. It's an examination."

"And you can read this?" Maureen pointed to the open pages of the book.

"Most of it."

"Brian!" She sat down next to him. "But how?"

"Did I not tell you, the Rothmans' daughter is a teacher? She's returned now, and gives me lessons every afternoon when my work is done."

"You didn't tell me. Can you even read a newspaper?"

Brian's answer was interrupted by the sound of heavy footsteps on the stairs. Maureen turned in her chair and started when someone knocked loudly on the door. That wouldn't be Mrs. Duffy. She hesitated and then went to the door.

"Good evening, miss. The O'Connors live here?"

Two men, both of them tall, loomed in the doorway. Before Maureen could say anything they stepped past her and came in.

One of the men went over to Brian. "Hard at work there, sonny?"

"Aye," Brian replied, regarding the two visitors curiously.

The other man stood near Maureen, his eyes roaming slowly around the room. He smiled. "Tell me, miss, are your mama and papa at home?"

Maureen glanced nervously at the first man, who was walking over to Mr. O'Leary's corner.

"No, sir."

"Well, can you tell me when either of them might be back? It's important."

"Mammy is still in Ireland. And our Da . . . our Da works in Pennsylvania. We've not seen him for many weeks."

"Now that's a real shame." The man touched a white envelope protruding from his jacket pocket. "We had a bit of money for your papa. Seems the gas works still owed him. But we can't give it to anyone else."

The second man had pulled back Mr. O'Leary's curtain and was eyeing the alcove's contents. "This could be his stuff," he said.

"That belongs to our lodger," Brian said, getting up from the table.

The man lifted the covers and mattress on the bed. "Hey now, what's this?" He picked up the old sock, knotted at one end and heavy with currency. He tossed it back and forth in his hands and winked at his partner.

"That's Mr. O'Leary's," Maureen's voice went shrill. "You put it back!"

The man ignored her and lifted a satchel from the floor. He rifled through it, then dumped the contents onto the bed. Three potatoes bounced down and rolled across the floor.

Brian was bending over to retrieve them just as Mr. O'Leary walked into the room.

"Janey Mack, what's this?" he said.

Both men turned.

"We're looking for Sean O'Connor, mister."

Mr. O'Leary spotted his money sock in the man's hand. He moved across the room. "If it's Sean O'Connor you're looking for, what are you doing with my belongings?"

"We thought he might have come back, and—"

"We told them Da wasn't here, that those were your things, Mr. O'Leary," Maureen declared. "They're not from the gas works at all."

One of the men leveled his eyes at Maureen. "No, miss? Now why would you say that?"

She took a step backwards. "Only . . . that it doesn't seem right, for Da to have money due. He was at the works but one week."

Mr. O'Leary went up to the man holding the money sock. "You've seen for yourself he's not here. Now I'm thanking you to get out."

The man tossed the sock down on the bed. "C'mon," he said to his partner. He turned again to Maureen. "You see your papa, miss, you tell him Otto Krebbs is looking for him. Got that?" The man grinned at his partner as they went out the door.

Maureen listened to their footsteps going down the stairs, then ran over to the window. The men came out of the building and stopped for a moment under the street lamp. The one named Krebbs took a small notebook from his pocket and wrote in it.

As they made their way up Oliver Street, Maureen saw a woman coming from the opposite direction. Mrs. Duffy paid the men no heed as she hurried by, and only when she stopped to draw out her latchkey did she give them a second glance.

20
A Livery on Broome Street

The kettle was hopping off the stove with its boiling. Maureen ran over and set it on the back plate.

"Oh," she said, her voice weak. That man, Krebbs, had frightened her. She wanted to see Mrs. Duffy as soon as possible.

Reaching for the tea tin, she spoke to Brian and Mr. O'Leary. "I just remembered that Mrs. Duffy wanted me to help her tonight with some mending. Her eyes are troubling her."

The tin slipped through Maureen's fingers and clattered to the floor, spilling the tea.

"Oh, the devil take it!" she cried.

"Ah, calm yourself," said Mr. O'Leary. "Don't be letting those men get the best of you." He crouched down and swept the spilled tea into his hand. "There, back in the tin with this, and no one the wiser."

"Thank you," Maureen said. "I'm afraid I'm all nerves tonight." She tried to be more careful as she measured out the tea.

Mr. O'Leary went down to the pump to wash. Maureen fidgeted with the teapot. Her hands trembled slightly as she poured a cup of tea for Brian. He looked at her questioningly and returned to his books.

"Brian? I'm going to see Mrs. Duffy now. When Mr. O'Leary returns, slice some of that rye loaf for him, hear?"

"O.K."

"And save a little for Paddy, in case he comes in hungry."

"O.K."

She could not help but smile. "O.K., O.K. Dear me, Brian O'Connor, you'll soon be more Yankee than Irish." She gave him a rap on the head as she went out the door.

Mrs. Duffy answered Maureen's knock. "Who's there?"

" 'Tis Maureen."

The lock slid back and Mrs. Duffy opened the door. "Come in," she said in a low voice. "Quick now, we've little time."

Maureen was puzzled. Spread out on the floor was an odd assortment: candle stubs, matches, woolen socks, a tin cup, a knife, biscuits and apples. Everything was heaped together on a blanket.

"It's good you're here, Maureen. I was about to come get you," Mrs. Duffy said. She pulled the corners of the blanket together to form a carrying sack.

"But what—?"

"Hush girl, and listen carefully. Your da is over on Broome Street, in Mr. Maxwell's livery. Never mind how he got there; I'll explain later."

Maureen gasped. "Is he all right?"

"Aye, he's safe for the moment."

Mrs. Duffy tied the blanket into a tight bundle and struggled to her feet. "Mick is driving a load of Thomas clocks up to Newburgh. Your da and two runaways, they'll be on his wagon, too."

"Oh, Mrs. Duffy!" Maureen ran over to the woman and hugged her.

"Now wait, you. 'Tis a long way to Canada. There are

safe stations in Newburgh and Albany, but after that the going will be chancy."

"Still—" Then Maureen remembered the slave who'd been caught at the produce market that morning. Mrs. Duffy was right; Da and the runaways weren't out of danger yet.

"Mick will be needing these supplies when he comes by the livery tonight," Mrs. Duffy said. "I think it's best that you take them, for I've been seen there too often of late."

"You mean go to the livery now?"

"I do. They're leaving tomorrow, before sunup. Mr. Maxwell is in the middle of Broome, just our side of the Bowery. Tell him you're returning this for Letty Trump. He'll take your meaning."

"Will I . . . can I see Da?"

"If Mr. Maxwell thinks it's safe, then you may. But mind, do as he says."

"I will." Maureen swallowed to ease the tightness in her throat. "Mrs. Duffy, the men who are after Da; they came to our room tonight."

"Ah, Mick said they'd be closing in." Mrs. Duffy handed Maureen the tied blanket. "Go the back way, through the hole in the fence. Take the alley as far as Coyle's Corner. From there follow along Chrystie. Less likely you'll come across anyone that way."

"I'll keep a watchful eye. And I'm thanking you, Mrs. Duffy, more than I can ever say."

Maureen went down the hall to the rear entrance of the lodging house. As she stepped into the shadowy yard the privy door swung open, its hinges creaking in the night air. For a moment her heart stopped. "God help me, 'tis only the wind," she breathed.

The alley was dark and she had to feel her way along its rutted path. When she reached Chrystie she kept close to the buildings, well away from the streetlights. Once she stopped, thinking she heard footsteps following her.

" 'Tis someone on his way home," she told her fluttering stomach. "Go on, now."

It was hard to think with so many questions crowding her head. How had Da known about the Underground Railroad? And what would he do once he reached Canada?

Something furry brushed her foot and she stifled a cry. A cat leaped from a window ledge in pursuit of a large rat that disappeared into the alley. Maureen waited a moment, then forced herself to continue on up the street.

Broome Street was up ahead. A livery sign could be seen in the middle of the block and when Maureen approached she heard two men talking. A man came out and went up the street.

She peeked around the stable entrance. A stooped, white-haired man was hanging tack gear on the wall. There appeared to be no one else in the livery.

"Mr. Maxwell?" Maureen's voice was muffled by the bales of hay lining the stable.

The man turned. His eyes went to the rolled-up blanket. "Good evening, miss."

"I'm bringing . . . Letty Trump's things."

"That's very kind of you." Mr. Maxwell shuffled to the door and glanced up and down the street. He motioned Maureen inside, then took the bundle and put it behind a large black carriage. "You arrived just in time, for I'll be closing soon."

"Mr. Maxwell? There's someone I very much want to see."

The man did not answer, but slowly pulled up the stakes holding the doors open. Once more he surveyed the street. The latch was then drawn over and secured.

Maureen waited, recalling Mrs. Duffy's admonition to do as Mr. Maxwell said. She could see from the man's gnarled hands and bent shoulders that the years had been hard on him. Yet his thin mouth was set in a kindly expression, and his eyes, when he turned to her, were surprisingly alert.

Mr. Maxwell pointed to the back of the stable. "Out there, in the chicken coop," he said quietly. "Be quick, though."

Maureen hurried through the stable into the yard. There was no lantern and the new moon offered little light.

A rustling noise came from the low shed near the stable. "Maureen, here," someone whispered. She could dimly see a figure crouched in the darkness.

She ran over to the coop and scrambled inside. The air was fetid, heavy with the stench of dung-littered straw. Da put his arms around her.

"You're all right?" she said.

"Aye. Thanks be to the Duffys."

"But what happened? How did you get here?"

"When you went to see Mrs. Duffy last night, I hid in the woodpile, with a plan to move on before dawn. The next thing I know, it's daylight, and Mick Duffy is standing over me.

" 'A man on the run has a certain look,' Mick says. 'Come inside.' Turns out he already knew what had happened, for Mrs. Duffy had told him. She came in and they started talking about 'safe stations' and 'runaways.' I couldn't make out half of it.

"Then Mick explained about the Underground Railroad going to Canada. I could come with them, he said, but it would be risky. Bounty hunters are trailing the slaves." Da paused and Maureen could hear the tenseness in his shallow breathing. " 'I'd be grateful to join you,' I told Mick."

It was quiet in the chicken coop. Da was a black profile against the shed walls. "Maureen," he said, his voice husky, "about Mammy. Let's not trouble her with news of this. Get Father Murphy to help you with the letters, and just say . . . I'm in the mines."

"What about Brian and Paddy? Should I—?"

A lantern light shone in the stable entrance. "Quickly, miss," Mr. Maxwell's voice urged, "time to go."

Da pushed open the little coop door. "Give the boys my love, and tell them . . . someday we'll all be together again." He hugged Maureen one last time. "God between you and harm," he whispered.

"Good-by, Da." The smell of the coal dust on his jacket hurt her throat. "I'll pray for a safe journey."

Maureen went across the yard into the pool of light cast by Mr. Maxwell's lantern. She did not look back for fear of tears coming.

21

Battery Park

Each night before going to sleep, Maureen thought about the wagonload of clocks and secret cargo Mick Duffy was taking to Newburgh. Where was Da sleeping tonight, she wondered. Was that man Krebbs still following him? And the runaway slaves, what of them? She prayed to St. Brigid to watch over the wagon and guide it safely to Canada.

The days crept slowly by. Wednesday, Thursday, Friday. Mrs. Duffy expected Mick back with news by Sunday. Sunday was also the day Edward Cooke had invited her to go to Battery Park. There was a quickening in her breast when she thought of the sailor. Why such nervousness over something as simple as a visit to the park?

Most mornings there was a thin layer of frost on the windows when Maureen awoke. By midday the sun tempered the chill November air, but such warming was only temporary.

Paddy came home one night wearing a pair of new brogans. They were large for him so he stuffed wads of newspaper into the toes until the shoes fit snugly. Walking proudly back and forth, he told Maureen he had won them in a game of craps and they were his to keep.

Soon Brian was wearing shoes as well, having allowed Mrs. Rothman to take him and a week's wages up to Houston Street to buy a factory pair. "Although they're not as carefully made as the cobbler's, they're suitable," Mrs. Rothman told him. "And better than nothing, come winter."

Brian's shoes squeaked loudly when he walked. Maureen thought he enjoyed the sound, judging from the smug look he gave the parishioners as she and Brian seated themselves at Mass. Maureen stared straight ahead, feeling rather conspicuous, but not because of Brian's shoes. After washing her hair this morning, she had stood before Mr. O'Leary's shaving mirror and tied a red ribbon in her hair, the ribbon being an extravagance she had allowed herself the day she bought yarn at the draper's. Now she wished she'd waited until after church to put the ribbon in.

It was hard to keep her mind on the Mass. Her thoughts jumped from Da, to Edward, to Ma, to that awful man, Krebbs. Twice Brian had to poke her to rouse her from the kneeler.

On the way out of church Maureen was surprised to see Paddy and some boys from Nolan's crowd standing at the back. Whacker himself was there, talking politely to Mrs. Maguire.

Paddy's hair lay neatly combed. Maureen raised her eyebrows. Most Saturday nights the boy didn't even come home; it was a miracle to see him at Mass on Sunday morning and neatly groomed at that.

Outside the church, Brian called to his brother.

"Hey, Paddy!"

"Hey, Brian," Paddy came over looking in a good humor. He grinned at Maureen. "Good morning."

"It's a treat seeing you here," Maureen said tartly. In a kinder tone, she added, "You look very nice, Paddy."

The boy adjusted Da's cap so it sat at a jaunty angle. "We're doing campaign work today."

"You're doing what?"

"The precinct." Paddy straightened his shoulders and nodded towards James Street. "You know, for the election, for Brendan Dooley."

"Oh?"

"We've got signs to put up in all the shops, telling people to vote. It's real important, 'cause the big swells uptown think they can beat Mr. Dooley."

"I could help if you want," Brian offered.

Paddy considered. "Nah. Whacker's particular about the guys who work for him. Besides, we got enough already." Paddy tilted his head at Maureen, his eyes noticing the red ribbon. "You going somewhere special today?" he asked.

The question flustered Maureen. She hadn't said anything to anyone about Edward's Sunday invitation. She'd meant to tell Brian but so much else had been on her mind, worrying about Da and all. Now she felt uncomfortable.

"Oh, well . . . I might be going down to the Battery today. I'm not certain."

"With that English sailor?"

"Aye . . . perhaps."

Paddy made a disagreeable noise in his throat.

"What's that supposed to mean?" Maureen said crossly.

"It means I remember the things the English did to us, that's what."

"But Paddy, Edward's not some *gombeen* landlord. And he risked his skin for you, on the boat."

Maureen knew from the look on her brother's face that there was no use in saying more. At a call from Whacker,

Paddy turned and went over to the park.

Brian stood with his hands in his pockets, looking glum. "Maybe I'll walk over to the Rothmans'. See if Miss Sarah has some more books for me."

"Brian, wait. You don't object to my seeing that English sailor, do you?"

Brian shrugged. "No."

"You'll not mind eating dinner a bit late today? Sure I'll still cook up those turnips for you."

"It's O.K. I can wait."

Maureen put her hand on Brian's shoulder. "Edward is very nice. You'll like him, Brian, I know you will."

"Well, I guess I'll see you later, Maureen."

Maureen watched the boy cross the street and go on toward Broome. She wished he had some friends in the neighborhood the same as Paddy. Not that she wanted Brian taking up with a rough crowd, but it troubled her to see him always going off alone.

Maureen walked back to Oliver Street. Mrs. Duffy was sitting on the front stoop and as soon as she saw Maureen she came bustling to meet her. "Good news!" she said, keeping her voice low. "Mick got in early this morning. Everything went smooth as silk as far as Newburgh. And there's a station near Albany that will help them get to Glens Falls. They'll be over halfway to Canada then."

Maureen gripped Mrs. Duffy's arms. "When will we know for certain that they're safe?"

"Maybe three weeks. Sometimes the word gets back sooner."

"Oh, tell Mr. Duffy I thank him."

"Ah, he knows that." Mrs. Duffy was looking at someone coming down the street. Maureen turned to see who it was.

"Hullo, Maureen."

"Edward. Why, good morning!"

The sailor stood back. "I'm early. I don't wish to interrupt . . ."

"That's all right, young man," Mrs. Duffy said. "I don't believe I know you from the neighborhood?"

"Ah . . . this is Edward Cooke, Mrs. Duffy," said Maureen. "He was a sailor on the *Western Star*. We met again, quite by accident, in the butcher shop uptown."

"Oh?" Mrs. Duffy gave Edward an appraising look. "It's a pleasure to meet you."

"How do you do, ma'am?"

"Mrs. Duffy runs the lodging house," Maureen said. "And a dear friend she is, as well."

"You've shore leave now, is that it?" Mrs. Duffy asked the sailor.

"No. I've quit the sea for a spell. Thinking of going out west."

"Soon?"

He hesitated. "Well, not *too* soon, with winter coming on and all." He looked at Maureen. "About this afternoon?"

"Oh, 'tis fine. I can go."

"Eh? Go where?" Mrs. Duffy raised her eyebrows. "Now don't keep an old woman guessing, Maureen," she scolded.

Maureen laughed. "Edward asked could I go to Battery Park with him this afternoon."

"Well, that's lovely. You have a pleasant time." Mrs. Duffy made a move toward her door.

"A good day to you, ma'am," said Edward. He turned to Maureen. "I'm not too early?"

"No, it's all right. I'm just getting back from church. You went to nine o'clock?"

"What?"

134

"Nine o'clock Mass, instead of ten?"

"No. I don't go to Mass."

"Oh." Maureen paused. "I quite forgot."

Edward studied her carefully. "If it's going to matter, lass, you might as well know right now; I've no church-going blood in me. None at all."

Maureen wasn't sure what to say. She glanced down awkwardly. "I . . . don't suppose it has to matter, does it?"

"No," he said, smiling slightly. He eyed her shawl. "It's right breezy down by the water. Will you be warm enough?"

"I think so."

"Well, then?"

They started off; Edward humming, hands in his pockets; Maureen smoothing back her hair, making sure the ribbon had not gone awry.

She felt happy. Da was safely on his way to Canada. Edward had called for her, just as he'd said he would. The fall day was crisp; the sky blue and cloudless.

"Is the Battery far?" she asked. "I've not been there before."

"Oh, you have," Edward teased. "Or very near it. The Star put in next to the Battery the day we landed. We've another mile or so."

A crowd of boys was playing stickball in the middle of Fulton Street. Men stood around in neatly ironed shirts, hair slicked back, faces clean, waiting for the local pubs to open. Young girls sat on the stoops, minding small children while their mothers prepared Sunday dinners of boiled beef or mutton.

At Whitehall Street Edward pointed up ahead. "That's the park, farther on where those trees are."

The Battery was a large green, graced by willow oaks and hawthorns going all the way to the seawall. The stone

135

fortress of Castle Garden stood to one side. The park was crowded with Sunday strollers and the refreshment vendors were doing good business in spite of the cool weather.

Maureen waited while Edward bought two sarsaparillas and some peanuts. All the benches were occupied so they sat on the grass watching the passersby. Two boys ran down the esplanade, rolling hoops and narrowly missing an organ grinder as he moved through the crowd. The organ grinder's monkey held his hand out to Edward, begging for a peanut.

Edward pointed to the seawall. "Want to go watch those schooners come in?"

It was windier near the water. Maureen pulled up her shawl, wrapping it around her shoulders. She saw how Edward paid close attention to the ships.

"What age were you when you went to sea?" she asked him.

"If you count from when I was with my pa, maybe four years old. Pa was a fisherman, off Southport."

"And then?"

"He drowned, going out one night to help a sinking trawler. My brother Jack and I were sent to Liverpool to live with an aunt. Our ma . . . she died when Jack was born."

Edward's eyes were thoughtful. "Aunt Lillie had enough trouble and didn't want any more. She hired me out to the mills. One day I decided to run away and stowed myself on a cargo brig. Gorblimy, if it wasn't bound for Australia!"

"Oh, my. Were you found out?"

"Indeed I was, when we were three days at sea. But the mate was a bonny fellow; said if I worked hard, he'd go easy on me.

"I've been on a ship ever since; mostly the China route.

136

Only signed for the *Star* at the last minute. Lars and I had missed our regular sailing on account of having yellow-jack fever."

Maureen stared quietly out at the whitecaps that came skimming across the water.

"What are you thinking?" Edward asked her.

"Of my ma. Sometimes I wonder if I'll ever see her again. It saddens me, hearing of you going to sea so young, with no ma or pa to care about you."

She turned and looked at him. "Do you still miss the sea, Edward?"

"Sometimes. Do you still miss Ireland?"

"I do, sometimes. 'Tis hard to leave a place you've known all your life."

He nodded, then reached over and took her right hand, holding it out flat in his palm. Her hand was red and chapped from the hours spent in the Cabot laundry tubs. He lightly stroked her fingers.

"You work hard," he said.

She noted a horny bump on his thumb where the nail had been torn away. "And you, the same," she replied.

He took her other hand and held it, not saying anything, but looking at her in that way he had, serious, and a bit questioning. Standing so near him, she could see how the years at sea had bleached his eyebrows until they were the color of sand.

"Maureen, it seems I've known you a long time," he said.

"I was thinking that myself, just now."

He brushed a lock of hair away from her face. "I'm very fond of you."

Something joyful and warm stirred inside her. "And I, of you, Edward," she said.

He put his arms around her then, and kissed her.

Maureen closed her eyes, feeling his face against her own. His skin held the faint scent of bayberry soap.

The sun moved toward the horizon. Visitors gathered up their picnic baskets and made their way across the green to the park gates. It was nearly dusk when Maureen and Edward began walking back to Oliver Street.

22
Father Murphy's Letter

The lamplighter nodded to Maureen and Edward as they turned into Oliver Street. They were walking arm in arm, holding each other close both for warmth and for the pleasure of it.

"Good evening, Tim," Maureen said, feeling a little out of breath. The walk up from the Battery had been at a good pace.

Tim bowed slightly as he lifted his cap. "Good evening to you. Getting dark early these nights."

"It is, indeed."

Maureen looked up at the O'Connors' window.

"Poor Brian, he'll be wondering about his turnips," she said to Edward.

"I didn't realize how late it was. Tell me, miss, do you always steal the hours from the day, and no warning?"

Maureen waggled her finger in a scolding manner. " 'Twas not only my doing, sir, but yours as well."

Edward put his arms around Maureen and held her snug against the lodging house. He kissed her forehead, the tip of her nose, her mouth.

"Oh, Edward," she murmured, "today was lovely. As lovely a day . . . as ever I've known."

They stood in the shadows, holding each other, for a long time. It was hard to say good-by.

Tim the Lamplighter took out his pipe as he approached the lodging house. He pretended not to notice Maureen and Edward.

"I must go," the sailor said at last. "Good night, Maureen."

"Good night, Edward. God bless."

Edward turned and ran up the street. When he reached the corner he stopped to wave. Maureen waved back. In the glimmer of light she could see Tim's amused expression while he rekindled his pipe.

"And good night to you as well, Tim the Lamp," she called gaily. Her cheeks were burning as she went up the stairs of the lodging house. "My heart," she sighed, "I've never been this way before."

Maureen paused at the landing to smooth back her hair. The sound of voices came from the room and she stepped closer to give a listen. It was Mr. O'Leary and—who else? Ah, of course, Father Murphy, making his monthly parish call. She straightened her shawl and went in.

Mr. O'Leary and the priest were at the table. Brian and Paddy sat together on the bed. Maureen looked at them and knew immediately that something was wrong.

Father Murphy stood up. "Maureen, good evening. It's well you're home, at last."

Maureen looked quickly at Mr. O'Leary. His eyes were sad as he rose and offered his chair. "Here, lass, sit down."

She moved slowly, fear clutching her innards. *Dear God, something terrible has happened to Da.*

Father Murphy's pink face was not up to the task before him. "Maureen," he said, "I've a letter. We . . . wanted to wait until you were here, before opening it. It was delivered special, to the presbytery. 'Tis from Ireland."

Having said this, Father Murphy reluctantly drew from his vest pocket a white envelope bearing a black border.

Brian came over to Maureen's chair. "It's to Da, from Uncle Owen," he said tearfully.

"Oh, Brian."

Mr. O'Leary reached across and touched her shoulder. "Would you be wanting Father to read it, Maureen?"

She nodded, seeing only a blur of black and white, of priest and envelope.

> *Killorgan, County Waterford*
> *Ireland*
> *2 October, 1847*
> *Dear Sean,*
>   *It is with a heavy heart I must tell you of your Mary's dying. Her consumption worsened sorely and took her from us. She went peacefully, with Father Cleary at her side, and will be buried on the hill outside Killorgan, next to your Rosheen. God keep their souls in Heaven.*
>   *I wish you to know that her last words were of you and the children, of her joy that you had found a new life in America.*
>   *Our cottage is the emptier now, with the little ones asking for their auntie. She was ever telling them one of Grandfar's stories.*
>   *Fiona and I send our love and deep sympathy. May God be with you.*
>   *Your brother-in-law,*
>   *Owen McLaughlin*

Father Murphy put the letter on the table. "It's sorry I am, children. You'll be wanting to write to your da, and tell him."

Maureen sat in the chair, unable to answer. She stared

141

at the black-bordered pages and the careful script. "Oh, Mammy," she whispered.

"I will pray for her soul," the priest said, putting on his hat. "Good night, then. And God bless you all."

The priest departed and the room was quiet. Brian stood next to Maureen, tears rolling down his cheeks. Paddy sat silently on the bed.

"There's comfort in knowing she went peacefully, and with a glad heart," Mr. O'Leary offered.

Maureen's hands twisted in her lap. What Mr. O'Leary said was true. Ma knew nothing of the trouble in the mines, or that Da had fled to Canada. She hadn't heard about the nights Paddy came home smelling of beer, or of the nights he had not come home at all.

Tears filled her eyes. But now Ma would never learn that Brian was becoming a fine scholar. Such news would have pleased her so. And what of Edward? Maureen could never tell her mother about the tall young sailor with eyes the color of the sea.

There was a soft rap at the door and Nora Duffy came in.

"Maureen. Boys. I just heard from Father Murphy. I'm very sorry."

Paddy was alone on the bed and Mrs. Duffy went to sit beside him. She put her arm on his shoulder. "It's hard losing your mother. I think she must have been proud of her children coming to a new land the way they did, so brave and all."

Paddy kept his head down, holding his body stiff against Mrs. Duffy.

"It's no shame to cry, Paddy," she said gently.

The boy jerked away. "Ma wouldn't have died if it wasn't for the English. Them taking everything, leaving us to starve."

He jumped up and went around the table, facing

Maureen. "You should know that! You, out with that sailor!"

Maureen reared back.

The boy was trembling. He started towards the door and Mrs. Duffy called to him.

"Paddy, the English have done Ireland many wrongs, I'll not argue that. But listen, boy. Their greatest wrong was in teaching us how to hate. 'Twas a lesson we learned well." Her voice softened. "Was that your mammy's way? To hate others so?"

Paddy's eyes glittered. "Ma's dead. I'll not be forgetting why." He ran out the door, slamming it hard behind him.

Mrs. Duffy stared at the floor. "Poor fellow. All that sorrow just hurting inside him. 'Tis easier, sometimes, to turn it into anger."

Brian sat at the table, holding the black-bordered envelope. Queen Victoria's stern visage stared out from the ochre postage stamp.

"All these weeks Ma has been dead," he said, "and we not knowing."

Maureen went to her brother and put her arm around him.

That night she lay awake a long time. Paddy did not come home and her heart was doubly sad, thinking of what he had said.

There was an expression Ma used when someone was leaving on a long journey. How did it go? "May we meet again, in Ireland, or in Heaven." That was it . . . "in Ireland, . . . or in Heaven."

She took comfort in the words and closed her eyes.

23
A Winter Day

December came down from the north, bringing a winter storm that buried New York under two feet of snow. Maureen struggled uptown as far as Bayard before deciding it was hopeless to try and reach the Cabots'. She had never missed a day of work, but surely Miss Trump would understand today. Even the omnibuses were not moving. Maureen's feet felt numb as she turned back toward Oliver Street.

If it were not so cold, she would have found the snow quite beautiful. It decorated the littered alleys and draped the tenements in soft, white dress. New York was brilliant in the morning light. But a scarf and shawl did little to keep her warm, even with the cast-off woolen sweater from Miss Trump. Her teeth chattered as she retraced the steps she had made in the snow.

From up ahead came the sound of scraping shovels. Some boys were clearing the snow from around Mooney's Tobacco Shop. Across the way, another crew was finishing a path to Coyle's Corner.

Maureen recognized the crew as Whacker Nolan's gang. Paddy was not among them; since Brendan Dooley's

144

election as alderman Paddy spent much of his time at Dooley's headquarters over on the Bowery. The man had taken a liking to the boy and used him to run messages or do other odd jobs. Maureen was glad, for she respected Mr. Dooley. But Paddy's bitterness toward Edward had not changed and this sorely troubled her.

Edward urged Maureen to leave the boy alone, saying there was no use trying to change his mind. "He has to do it on his own, if it's to mean anything," Edward said. Perhaps that was true, thought Maureen. Thank goodness Brian had good wits in his head. He and Edward got on very well, as did Edward and Mr. O'Leary. Mr. O'Leary's maps of the states and territories were of great interest to the sailor; there was much talk of canals, rivers and routes west whenever Mr. O'Leary and the sailor were together.

Mrs. Duffy came trudging through the snow with her market basket. At first Maureen barely recognized her. She wore a red scarf wrapped around her head, covering her face from eyes to chin.

"Ah, Maureen." Mrs. Duffy's voice was muffled by the scarf. "Devil carry the word, it's winter sure."

"Indeed it is. I'm near frozen, and there's no getting uptown to the Cabots'."

"Not to worry. Little is happening in New York today."

"Are the shops open?" Maureen noted Mrs. Duffy's market basket.

"Not likely. But I'm off to get molasses and vinegar for Mick's sore throat. Mrs. Maguire will have something."

"Is the stale bread man coming this morning?"

Mrs. Duffy snorted. "In this weather?"

"Then I'm thinking it's a good day to bake a soda bread. Sure the heat from the stove will be welcome."

"Ah now, would you be trading a cup of tea for a warm slice?"

"I would, Mrs. Duffy. Best I move along now, or these feet will be lumps of ice. Come upstairs when you return."

No one was there when Maureen got back to the lodging house. She fed wood into the stove and welcomed the circle of heat that slowly spread into the room. She took the bag of flour and the soda jar down from the shelf, then poured the last of yesterday's buttermilk into a bowl. Good, there was just enough.

Brian's books, speller and writing pad were spread across the table where he'd left them before going to the Rothmans'. Morning and night now, his head was in the books. He talked to Mr. O'Leary about men Maureen had never heard of, poets and the like. And one would think Sarah Rothman a queen twice over, to hear Brian speak of her.

Maureen pushed the books aside to make room for kneading the bread. She shaped the dough into a round loaf, made an "x" across the top with a knife and put the bread in the oven.

Brian's pen lay next to the writing pad. Maureen picked it up, admiring the slender nib. She wondered if she could still print her name, or any of the other words the visiting hedgemaster had once taught her back in Ireland. She brushed the flour from her hands and dipped the pen into the jar of ink. A blob dribbled down onto the paper as she started the letter "M."

Slowly she formed the letters of her name. They were large and crooked next to Brian's fine hand, but she had not forgotten them.

Maureen opened one of the books. Rows of black letters swam before her eyes. The page might as well have been a smear of ink for all she could make of it. A kind of sadness came over her. It had to do with the books, the writing pen, with the way she felt when Edward and Mr. O'Leary

146

talked about things they'd read in the *New York Sun*. Or when Brian came home, flushed with anticipation, another book from Miss Sarah under his arm.

She wanted to read, too. And know how to write. Not just her name, but other things, the way Brian could.

There were slow footsteps coming up the stairs. That would be Mrs. Duffy. Maureen shoved the writing tablet under a book and went to the door.

"I tell you, I've never known a day so cold!" Mrs. Duffy lumbered in, her cheeks and nose a bright red.

Maureen moved two chairs up near the stove. "Sit here, Mrs. Duffy," she said, and put the kettle on.

Mrs. Duffy got out a packet of tea, sniffing the bread approvingly.

Maureen was soon pouring two cups of tea. For many weeks she'd wanted to ask Mrs. Duffy about something. Perhaps this was a good time to do so. "Mrs. Duffy? I've a question."

"Eh?"

"Well, since that day in the warehouse with Amos and Job, I've been wondering how you and Mick ever took up with Quakers like Letty Trump."

Mrs. Duffy sagged slightly in her chair. "Oh, my. 'Tis a long story, that one. I'll need my tea." She took a swallow from the steaming cup.

"This much I'll tell: Back in Ireland, Mick was with the rebels. The English were looking for him, and after a raid on their barracks an informer turned him in. He was taken off to Dartmoor Prison, and I thought I'd never see him again. Six long years passed, and then didn't Mick manage to hide himself under the charnel wagon as it went to the prison graveyard one night! Nearly dead himself, he was, from the beatings and rotten food. But he got away.

"A ship captain, a Quaker, took pity on Mick and let

147

him stow away in his ship. Now mind, Maureen, the Quakers are peaceable. They didn't approve of Mick's fighting ways, but they didn't like what the English had done to him, either. So the captain agreed to take him to America.

"At the end of the journey, he said Mick could pay him by giving the same help to another man. 'You'll have your chance one day,' the captain said.

"I came to America not long after, and we married. One morning Mick was working the docks and found a runaway slave hiding in an empty hogshead. The poor man was covered with whipping scars, and begged that he not be returned to his master. Mick remembered what the ship captain had said, and vowed to help the runaway. That's when we came to know Letty Trump."

Mrs. Duffy shook her head. "Those Quakers. It's a peculiar faith they have, if you ask me. But there's no people more kind, nor willing to give of themselves for others."

Maureen thought of Da and the wagon going to Canada. "Mrs. Duffy, if I can ever help the Underground Railroad, or those Quakers, will you tell me?"

Mrs. Duffy smiled rather wearily. She turned toward the door. "That sounds like your Brian and Mr. O'Leary on the stairs."

The man and boy came in the door, faces red, noses dripping.

"Maureen, I hoped you'd be here," Brian said. "I've some good news!"

"You bought a winter coat with fox-fur trim for your sister?" she teased.

Mr. O'Leary was beaming. He put his hands on Brian's shoulders. "Go on, lad, show her."

Brian reached under his jacket and pulled out an

envelope. "Miss Sarah gave me this. I got admitted to the Goodson Academy, Maureen! See here?" He held the letter out to her.

Maureen pushed it away. "Go on, old man. You know I can't read. What do you mean, 'got admitted'?"

"Remember the school Miss Sarah told me about? The one in Massachusetts?" He turned the letter around and read from it. " 'Books, lodgings and meals will be provided in exchange for the student's labor.' I can start the January term, and Mr. Rothman has agreed to give me extra work for the train fare."

Maureen stared at her brother. A dim recollection came to her: Brian talking of going away to a real school one day. She had thought it all wishful dreaming at the time.

"But Brian," she said weakly, "Massachusetts?"

"I know. It's a long way. Mr. O'Leary says there's trains from New York to Boston. Maybe you could come visit."

Maureen sat down. "It's just that with Da gone, and Paddy . . ." She couldn't find the right words to say.

"Maureen?"

She looked up at Mr. O'Leary. His eyes were moist. "It's a fine chance for the lad," he said. "We'll all miss him, myself as much as anyone. But think of it, your own brother going to an academy, a place for scholars. He does us proud."

Maureen blinked back her tears. How Ma would have smiled at such news. "I know. And proud I am, too. Only wishing Massachusetts was close by, is all."

24
Christmas in New York

Winter bit into New York with icy teeth and the city cowered beneath the fierce cold. Maureen and Edward no longer walked to the Battery on Sunday afternoons, preferring the warmth of the lodging house cookstove and the company of Brian and Mr. O'Leary instead.

"I've sent my Bridget the passage money," said Mr. O'Leary one Sunday. "The way things are in Ireland, I fear the children might not last till spring. Better to risk a winter crossing than none at all."

"You're still thinking of going to St. Louis, come spring?" asked Edward.

"I am. A booming town, good prospects. And with a mighty river on her doorstep, sure she's a place with a good future. Look here, Edward," Mr. O'Leary held up his map, "you could go down the Mississippi and out to sea. Why, you'd be right at home there, lad. You ought to come with us, I tell you."

Edward knew the river's whereabouts as well as did Mr. O'Leary. "Perhaps so. I'd like to see more of the country, that's certain."

Maureen listened to the talk of going west with misgiving. Mr. O'Leary was a good friend and one she would miss. If Edward also left New York . . . she did not wish to think of it.

Brian hunched over his writing pad, diligently working on another essay for Miss Sarah. All at once he stopped writing and looked up at Edward. "However did you go to school if you were off at sea so young?" he asked.

Edward chuckled. "There's every manner of teacher on a sailing ship, lad. The best I had was a boatswain named Harry Figg. Harry knew everything, and then a bit more. As soon as my watch was over, he'd sit me down and drill me like any master. We called the forecastle 'Harry's School.' "

"We didn't have a school in Ireland," said Brian. "But there were traveling schoolmasters coming 'round, setting up a hedge-school from time to time. Paddy and I would attend them . . . before the praties went bad."

"I learned to write my name," Maureen blurted out, "for the hedgemaster stayed with us once and taught me." She looked sheepishly at Edward. "I can't read, though. 'Twas never any school for girls." She turned to her knitting, keeping her head down. "Perhaps someday . . ." she began, but did not finish the sentence.

It was the day before Christmas. Miss Trump dismissed the staff early and Maureen was on her way home. Each servant had been given a bag of nuts and candies and Cook had presented Maureen with two mince tarts. Such goodies were welcome, indeed, for neither Maureen nor Mr. O'Leary had extra money to buy special food. To-morrow's dinner would be the usual boiled cabbage, boiled potatoes, and buttermilk.

Maureen was pleased that she'd managed to make a few small gifts to give on Christmas Day. Using leftover yarn, she'd knitted little woolen egg cozies. They were simple round "hats," pretty to the eye, and would keep a boiled egg warm on a cold morning. "Not that we've an abundance of eggs," she told herself ruefully.

Maureen neared Henry Street and saw Old Sal and her son, Perry, up ahead. They were sitting on the stoop, catching the winter sun. Perry held a piece of charcoal and a sketch pad and was drawing his mother.

As Maureen approached, Sal called out to her, "Maureen? I hear you flibberty-steppin' along, girl."

"Right you are," Maureen answered. She stopped to greet Sal's dog, Barney, and to observe Perry's work. The drawing showed Sal half-asleep, her tired body slumped against the step.

"My, Perry, 'tis a true likeness," Maureen said. "However did you learn to draw such?"

"Didn't learn," Perry replied. "Just do it."

"Show her the others," Sal said.

"These?" Maureen picked up the sketch pad lying on the stoop. There was Sal again, and Hickory, the iceman. And a sketch of the Henry Street buildings, and one of . . . "Perry, isn't this Battery Park?"

"Yup."

"But, it's wonderful. The ships coming alongside Castle Garden—they look to be moving."

Sal leaned back and chuckled. "Listen up, Perry. People see your work, they like it. You ought not to go throwin' it away."

Maureen clutched the sketch pad. "Throw away? This one?"

Perry shrugged. "That's just for practice. And anyway, I didn't get the trees proper."

Maureen held the drawing out and examined it. "They're perfect, to my eye." She hesitated. "Perry, if you're not wanting this, might I have it?"

152

The man smiled. "Oh, I reckon." He leaned over and put the letter "P" in the corner of the drawing. "Here you are, signed and all."

Maureen was beaming. "Thank you very much. You don't know how much this means. A Merry Christmas to you both! And to you, Barney, as well," she added, patting the dog.

Maureen hurried on to Oliver Street, her heart singing. She could give Edward the drawing of Battery Park as a special surprise!

Brian and Mr. O'Leary greeted her as Maureen came in the door.

"You must see what I have," Maureen said. She set down the bag of candies and the mince tarts. Brian eagerly moved toward them.

"No, no, Brian, *this.*" She smoothed the drawing out on the table. "See? Old Sal's son, Perry, drew it. I'm giving it to Edward for Christmas."

"Ah, Battery Park," said Mr. O'Leary. "Very nice, indeed."

Maureen noticed a large brown bag on the floor. "What's that?"

"Take a look," Mr. O'Leary said.

She bent over and loosened the wrapping. Inside was a fine, plump-breasted turkey.

"For us? But how did you—?"

" 'Twas not I, Maureen. A certain Padraic O'Connor was here."

"Paddy? But he can't afford such a bird. It must be fifteen pounds."

"It's a gift from Brendan Dooley."

"Really?" Maureen looked at the turkey again. " 'Tis a generous gift. Did Paddy say he'd join us then, for Christmas?"

"I asked him to. But he said he'll be busy. There's more

deliveries to be made, to widows and the like."

"I see." Maureen fingered the paper wrapping. She was sorry she'd not been at home when Paddy came by.

"We might invite the Duffys and your Edward to share the turkey with us," Mr. O'Leary said.

Maureen nodded. "A good idea."

Mr. O'Leary went to the window and looked out at the sky. Dark clouds were gathering in the east. He seemed uneasy.

"Is something the matter?" Maureen asked.

"There's a storm heading this way. It could mean bad weather out at sea."

"Oh, dear, of course. I quite forgot about your family. Pray God they're safe."

Maureen rose at dawn Christmas morning, for the turkey needed plucking and cleaning before being put in the oven to roast. She moved quietly around the cold room, taking care not to awaken Brian and Mr. O'Leary.

A snowstorm had come during the night, but by ten o' clock the sky was clear. Mr. O'Leary's spirits improved with the weather. He and Brian tidied the room while Maureen busied herself at the stove.

Toward midafternoon there was a knock at the door. In came Edward, a grin on his face. "Something smells mighty good," he said. "Half the neighborhood is outside, hoping to be invited up here."

Maureen looked nervously at the roasting turkey. "Oh, I hope I'm doing it proper," she said. "I've never cooked such before." The fat hissed as she dipped a rag into the pan and wiped the bird until it glistened.

Edward stood behind her and peered into the oven. "You didn't tell me we were having such fine fare, Maureen."

"I didn't know. The turkey was here when I got home yesterday. A present from the new alderman, Mr. Dooley. Paddy delivered it."

"Ah. Then he'll join us today?"

Maureen shook her head. "No. He has other plans, as usual."

"I'm sorry . . ."

Maureen thought a moment. "Paddy knows he's wrong, Edward, I'm sure. But there's so much stubbornness in him, he'll not admit it."

Nora and Mick Duffy appeared in the doorway. "My belly can't believe what my nose is telling," said Mick. "*This* is a Christmas dinner!"

Maureen smiled. All eyes were on the turkey as she brought it to the table. "Best to let it sit till the juices settle, Cook always says."

Mrs. Duffy helped Maureen with the gravy while Edward and Mr. O'Leary brought a packing box up from the yard to use as an extra chair.

When everything was ready Maureen held the knife and fork out to Mrs. Duffy. "Please, would you do the carving? I'll be all thumbs."

"Oh, girl, I'm not the one to ask. These hands have had little practice carving turkeys."

"Ah-hem."

Maureen blinked as Edward came behind her and took the knife and fork. He tested the blade against his finger, then stepped over to the table. There was a gush of steam as the fork plunged into the golden breast. No one said a word as he cut sideways and down, laying out the meat in neat, thin slices.

"Well, I declare!" Mrs. Duffy's admiration was repeated around the room.

Edward took a small bow. "A ship captain dines well,

155

even if his crew does not. A sailor working the galley learns to carve proper, or else."

The turkey was perfectly done. Mrs. Duffy served up the stuffing she'd made and the pungent smell of sage wafted across the table.

"That's as fine a bird as ever was cooked," Mr. O'Leary announced.

"Agreed!" chorused Edward and Brian.

Everyone ate heartily. Even Mick Duffy, generally quiet and sober-faced, smiled good-naturedly when Maureen insisted he share the wishbone with Mrs. Duffy. "Now what would that woman be wishing for?" he asked. "Hasn't she everything she needs, including a decent husband?"

When dinner was over Mr. O'Leary got up from the table. "I've a need to lighten my satchel," he said, going over to his bed. He went around the table, placing a small gift before each person. When he came to Maureen he gave her a writing pad, pen and jar of ink. "You'll put these to good use someday, I'm thinking."

"Why, Mr. O'Leary, many thanks," she said, recalling the day she'd used Brian's pen. Mr. O'Leary must have known.

Other gifts were exchanged: a pencil box for Brian, a chocolate bar for the Duffys, a map of the Western Territories for Edward. Brian took the knitted egg cozy Maureen had made him and put it over his nose. "A double use, eh?" he laughed. "For winter days?"

Maureen glanced sideways at Edward. He was holding something behind his back as he came toward her.

"This is for you, Maureen. It's nothing fancy." He held out a soft green woolen hat with matching mittens.

"Oh, Edward, what a lovely color. And just what I've been needing in this cold weather." Maureen put on the

156

hat and admired herself in Mr. O'Leary's shaving glass. The green wool was very like the color of her eyes. " 'Tis a perfect fit."

She went to the cupboard where she'd hidden Perry's drawing. "Now I have something for you."

"Gorblimy, it's Battery Park," Edward said, unrolling the sketch. He took Maureen's hand. "It's a place I'll always remember."

Maureen moved close to Edward, her contentment nearly complete. If only Paddy and Da were here, then she would be truly happy.

25
Chatham Square

Sarah Rothman came by to talk with Maureen about Brian and the academy in Massachusetts.

She was a slender woman with quick, intense eyes. Although rather plain, she had a gracefulness that Maureen admired.

"Your brother has a fine mind," she said to Maureen. "I've never come across someone so eager to learn. Mama said he was at Papa's books from the very start. And such a memory!"

"Our grandfar was a *seanachie*."

"I beg your pardon?"

"In Ireland . . . 'tis a keeper of legends and happenings. He goes about the country, from village to village, telling the stories to all who gather 'round."

"A walking library," Sarah Rothman said with a laugh.

"Maureen, I want you to know the Goodson Academy is an excellent school. Boys of every faith attend, and everyone is expected to earn his keep. Brian will learn cooking and cleaning as well as Plato and Shakespeare."

"That's grand. If only the school wasn't so far away."

"I know. I also wish it were nearer. Brian has promised

me he will write to you each week."

Maureen thought about the paper tablet and pen from Mr. O'Leary. She had practiced with them, printing the few words she knew.

"Miss Sarah? Is there someplace in New York that I could learn to read and write?"

"Brian tells me you work uptown, as a washerwoman. Is that every day?"

"Except for Sunday."

"Well, there is a night school on Oak Street, not far from here. Let me see if it might have a place for you."

"It's a real school?"

"Indeed. And there are many like yourself in attendance. Men and women who work days and go to school nights."

"If I could learn to read and write, I'd be ever grateful to you, Miss Sarah."

"Oak Street is a small school, and already crowded. I can't promise there's room. But I'll go see Mr. Mellen right away, and let you know."

The Cabots were giving a New Year's party.

Maureen was tired from doing three extra baskets of linens. She stopped to admire the party decorations in the dining room, but of greater interest were the cakes and dainties lining the pantry shelves: vanilla toffees, hickorynut cake, cranberry pudding. How Cook could prepare such delights without constantly tasting them was a wonder to Maureen. If she was the cook, her skirt would be bursting its seams. Sighing wearily, she donned sweater, shawl, and the new woolen hat from Edward.

"Happy New Year, Maureen," Cook called to her.

"To you, the same," Maureen replied. She waved to Millie and went out the door.

Her bones ached as she made her way down the lane. All at once her tiredness vanished. Edward was waiting by the Cabots' gate.

"You're off early?" she called, running to meet him.

"Blimey, we never started. Lars was at the rum by ten o'clock. The others joined soon after." Edward's arm went around Maureen's waist as they walked along.

"Did you celebrate, too?" she asked him.

"Oh, a little. I'm fond of rum now and then. But more fond of Irish washerwomen."

"Go on with you. That's only the rum talking."

"It is not. It's Edward Cooke speaking the truth from his heart."

They hopped the omnibus and rode down to the Bowery. Lamps glowed from the alehouses as darkness settled over the city, but it was too early for serious revelry. The streets were quiet. In the dusky light some children played soldier's-fort in the excavation near Chatham Square.

"By this time next week, Brian will be gone," Maureen said. There was sadness in her voice.

"Now, Maureen, don't be fretting. You're not losing him."

"I know. But I'll miss that old man of a boy. At least when Mr. O'Leary's family arrives the flat won't be so lonely."

"Any word from them yet?"

"No. And Mr. O'Leary is filled with worry. He fears they've had trouble out at sea."

Edward rubbed his shoulder. "Hmm, I think they'll be here soon. I feel it in my sailor's bones."

"Really? Oh, Edward, I hope you're right."

Suddenly a child's cry startled Maureen. She turned and saw two boys scrambling down the dirt mound at the excavation site.

160

"Help, mister! Timmy fell in the water!"

"Water? Where?" Edward ran toward the boys.

"Down the pit. The ice broke!"

The boys went back up the mound with Edward and Maureen following. At the top they looked down into a cavity that had filled with water. A thin sheet of ice lay on the surface.

"We was playing king-of-the-hill," said the older boy. "Timmy rolled down!"

Edward and Maureen hurried to the bottom of the slope. Off to the left a frantic splashing could be heard. Edward threw off jacket and boots and groped his way into the icy water.

"I don't see him. Hallo? Timmy?" Edward gasped as the bottom gave way and he was in the water up to his chin.

Maureen heard a grunting sound. A figure appeared beside Edward and two small arms lunged at his neck, clinging to him and pulling him underwater.

"Edward, take this!" Maureen waded into the pit and tossed her shawl out, keeping hold of one end.

Edward struggled to free himself from the boy's grasp. Then he grabbed for the shawl and held onto Timmy with his other hand. Slowly he pulled toward the pit edge and staggered out of the water. Timmy was coughing and gasping for air. All at once he began crying.

"A good sign if he's breath enough to cry," Edward said. "But he'll freeze to death if we don't get him warmed up."

His teeth chattered as he called to Timmy's companions. "Ahoy, lads! Where does this one live?"

The other boys had watched the rescue in frightened silence. Now that the worst was over they began laying blame.

"It was you what pushed him, Andy. Ma will have your hide."

"Liar! You made him fall."

"Bother who's fault it was," Maureen said, seizing the older boy. "Quickly now, where does Timmy live?"

"We's jes' over there. Mott Street."

"Maureen, my boots and jacket, get them. Put the jacket over the boy. Hurry!" Edward shivered uncontrollably as he pulled on his boots. With stiff hands, he gathered Timmy into his arms.

At the top of the mound the boys pointed across Chatham Square. "That way," they said.

Edward and Maureen began running. Halfway down the block a woman was standing out on a front stoop. The two older boys hung back as she came down the steps.

"Timothy Garvey," the woman hollered, approaching Edward. "I told you to stay clear of that digging!" She threw Edward's jacket aside and took the boy from him. "Wet as a duck, and those your Christmas pants, too."

She whacked Timmy and reached for the two other boys. "Get inside, you need a good switching!"

The boys slunk up the steps, hands covering their bottoms. At the door the woman turned to Edward and Maureen. "Stand there in them wet clothes, you'll be frozen by morning." Without another word she slammed the door.

"Why, I never!" Maureen said.

"Come on, she's right."

"But Edward—"

"Never mind!" He put on his jacket and they hurried back across the square toward Oliver Street. Maureen's feet were icy; her wet shawl was rigid from the cold. She realized poor Edward was soaked from head to toe.

Finally they came to the lodging house and stumbled up the stairs. Edward's hair was standing out in stiff little strands and his skin had a bluish cast.

Mr. O'Leary opened the door. "What's happened to you?" he said with alarm.

"Boy . . . in . . . water." Edward tried to speak but his lips would not move.

Brian jumped up from his chair. "I'll run down to Larkin's for some whiskey," he said.

"Aye, boy, hurry!" said Mr. O'Leary. "Edward, out of those clothes. Maureen, heat up the stove, and get a blanket."

Maureen opened the stove box and threw wood on the fire. She ran to her bed and gathered up the blanket. As she turned around Mr. O'Leary was pulling off Edward's undershirt. She saw that his back was scarred with ugly red welts.

Maureen covered her mouth. A memory suddenly came to her: that day on the *Star*, when she had heard the swift cracking sounds near the forecastle . . . a sailor was being flogged. Now she knew why Da was so upset. The sailor was Edward Cooke, being punished for taking lemons from the pantry.

"My God," she said, going to him and gently putting the blanket over his back. "You never told me," she whispered.

He shook his head, too cold to answer.

Mr. O'Leary moved Edward closer to the stove. In a few minutes the color was returning to his face. "Ah, that's a bit better now," said Mr. O'Leary. "You had me worried."

Brian came running in the door, clutching a glass of whiskey. "Mr. Larkin says mix it with hot tea and honey, the better to thaw him." The boy's eyes were wide with excitement. "And something else! There's a woman with five children coming up the street. Mr. O'Leary, I'm thinking it might be your missus!"

Mr. O'Leary bolted upright. "Where, Brian, where?"

From out in the hallway came the sound of whimpering voices, and a woman hushing them. Mr. O'Leary leaped to the door.

There stood a tall, dark-haired woman, a traveling bag in each hand. Around her, wan-faced and weary, were five small children.

"Why, Christy O'Leary," the woman said with surprise, "you've grown a beard."

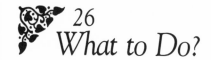

26
What to Do?

Maureen, Edward and Miss Sarah went to the train station to see Brian off. He looked woefully small inside the topcoat Mrs. Rothman had bought him. In one hand was the sailcloth grip Edward had made and in the other a bag of eats put up by Mrs. Duffy: bread, boiled eggs, raisins, cheese, apples.

"At least you'll not go hungry," Maureen joked to hide her sadness.

"Remember, Brian, Mrs. Whittier will meet you at the station. Don't go wandering off." Miss Sarah appeared to be as nervous as Brian.

"We'll all be waiting for your first letter," Edward said.

"Perhaps I'll soon be able to write to you," Maureen added.

Brian's face brightened. "Sure that will be grand, Maureen."

They all jumped when the train whistle blew its final call.

"Good luck, lad." Edward shook Brian's hand.

"God bless you," Maureen said, hugging her brother.

Brian clung to Maureen for a moment before turning to Sarah Rothman. "Good-by," he said. "I thank you for all you've done, Miss Sarah. I won't forget your generous heart as long as I live."

"Go on, now. You'll miss the train and then what will we do?" Miss Sarah dabbed at her eyes.

The engine belched black smoke clouds as it slowly pulled away. Brian pressed his face to the window, and then he was gone.

With the arrival of Bridget O'Leary and her five children, the little room on Oliver Street took on the appearance of a noisy, crowded stable. It was difficult to move without colliding with a small child. At the end of each day, wee faces waited at the window, watching for Mr. O'Leary's return. In his pockets they were sure to find peanuts or perhaps some sausage rolls to share. The smell of the knackers bothered the children not a whit.

Bridget O'Leary was a straightforward, friendly woman. She took an interest in Maureen without being nosy, and she got on well with Edward. She agreed with her husband that the sailor should consider moving to St. Louis with them. "Christy says there's all kinds of jobs waiting," she stated. "Besides, this New York is such a crowded place; I want to live where I can see the sky."

Maureen began attending the Oak Street School four nights a week. Miss Sarah was right, the school was crowded. But Mr. Mellen seemed a careful teacher, making sure that each student got some attention. It was hard, after a day at the Cabots', to sit in the stuffy classroom and concentrate on the evening's lesson. Yet there was also an excitement in being there, in seeing strange words become familiar. Maureen was especially happy when Mr. Mellen held up a newspaper and told the class, "You will be able to read every page of this some day."

One night Sarah Rothman was in front of the classroom

when Maureen came out. "Mr. Mellen tells me you're doing very well," she said. "I'm not surprised."

The compliment pleased Maureen. "By the way, we had another letter from Brian this week," she said.

"And I, as well. I think he's quite happy at the school."

"Perhaps a bit homesick, but loving the books. Did he tell you he learned to bake bread?"

"Not only did he bake it, he ground the flour as well." Miss Sarah laughed, but then her face turned serious. "Keep up the good work in school. And remember, Maureen, there's no need to be hiding your brains under a washtub. Do something with them. Good night, now."

On the way home, Maureen wondered what Miss Sarah meant by "do something." She wanted to write letters and read the *Sun;* that was "something" as far as she was concerned.

Often when Maureen got home at night, Edward and Mr. O'Leary would be talking about opportunities out west, or studying their maps. Tonight was the same: the O'Leary children were asleep on the floor, Mrs. O'Leary sat with her knitting, Edward and Mr. O'Leary stood at the table, a new map spread before them.

"Hullo. How was it tonight?" Edward asked when Maureen came in the door.

She held out her speller. "See? Only one mistake."

"Ah, very good." He smiled and took her hand.

She looked down at the map. "At it again, the two of you?" She tried to sound amused, but in truth, all the talk of going west made her heart ache. She did not want to think of Edward being so far away.

The first hint that spring might be approaching came from the gradually lengthening days as March gave way to April. Yet winter retreated only a few steps, leaving behind a shroud of gray mist.

167

Sunday the sky cleared enough to allow a walk to the Battery. Edward brought along his oil slicker in case of rain and he and Maureen set out at a brisk pace.

The only visitors to the park were others like themselves, eager for a breath of fresh air after too long a winter. Maureen and Edward stood by the seawall, looking out at the choppy water while the damp wind came at them.

Edward closed his eyes. "Ah," he said, taking a deep breath.

"You and your salt air," Maureen teased.

"I told you, it gets in the blood."

"Then you'll miss it if you go west," she said, less joking.

"I'll miss someone else more." He turned to her. "Maureen? I want to talk to you." He took her hand and led her to a nearby bench.

"You see, Mr. O'Leary and I've been thinking we might work together in St. Louis, doing carpentry and the like. As you know, it's a thriving town."

Edward paused and rubbed his hands across his knees. "Mrs. O'Leary could use some help for the trip west, getting settled with the children and all. We wondered . . . if you might come along?"

"You mean, *move* to St. Louis?"

"Well, yes. You'd live with the O'Learys. I'd get a room somewhere. We'd be able to see each other, and—"

He gripped his knees. "I might as well say it out. What I really hope is that you'll marry me one day. I know there's the matter of religion, and Paddy, and your pa. But I'm saying it anyway: I love you, Maureen. I want you for my wife."

She looked at him, at his quiet gray eyes and his finely-chiseled English nose. "Edward Cooke," she said, "I've wondered what I'd do if you left New York. I've told myself we'll have to part someday but the very thought of it saddens me. Still, I can't just up and leave . . ."

The sky began spitting rain.

"Why is it I always seem to be with you in the rain?" Edward said, pulling her close under the slicker.

"Mr. O'Leary is going to talk to Paddy, Maureen. He says the lad can move west with us, if he wants. Maybe your pa could come to St. Louis someday, too. And Brian can visit, though it's a good deal farther from Boston, I admit."

"Edward, I do want to be with you, but there's so much to think about."

"You don't have to decide right away. I know it's not easy, after all that's happened these past months."

Edward clapped his hand to his head. "Oh, another thing. Mr. O'Leary says St. Louis is sure to have a school for immigrants and the like. So you'd not have to give up your lessons."

Maureen thought about the Oak Street School with its smell of chalk dust.

"That's good to know," she replied. "For I'll not quit school until I can read the *New York Sun* from front to back."

Maureen went to see Mrs. Duffy.

"If it weren't for Paddy, I think I'd go west with the O'Leary's straightaway," she said. "But if he won't come, I don't see how I could leave him. He's still a boy."

"A boy trying hard to be a man."

"True enough."

"Maureen, one might say that in a way, Paddy has left you. Remember, it was his choice to quit staying at Oliver Street. I could be wrong, but I don't think he'd take well to being under you and the O'Learys out there in St. Louis, the bunch of you telling him what to do. That boy has a mind of his own.

"I saw him the other day, bringing a food cart from Mr.

Dooley around to the Kennedys' on account of Mr. Kennedy's lungs going bad. Oh, I'll give Dooley this: he looks out for folks no one else in the city cares about. Anyway, Dooley knows that Paddy's not a common ruffian; he puts the boy to good use. And keeps an eye out for him, too."

"It's hard to know what to do, Mrs. Duffy. So much has changed since we came to America. 'Twas different . . . in Ireland."

"I know. Maureen, I've a question. Do you love Edward?"

Maureen looked up. The question had never been asked before, but she knew her answer. "Yes, I do. Very much."

"Tell me, is he a Protestant?"

"He's no religion at all." Maureen could feel the heat coming to her cheeks as she spoke. She stood and faced Mrs. Duffy. "But I'll tell you something. Edward Cooke is as good a man as there can be, religion or no! And I've no patience anymore with the talk around here of being Irish, or English, or Catholic, or . . . or Jewish. Why, just last week Mrs. Maguire asked me, 'Did that Jew-man Rothman cheat Brian on his wages?' Imagine, Mrs. Maguire! Her with her fat thumb on the scale if you don't watch her."

Mrs. Duffy held up her hands. "Calm yourself, girl. I've nothing at all against Edward. He's a fine young man. I'm only saying be sure of your feelings. It's not easy, going against the old ways. We've troubles enough in this life without taking on more."

"Oh, Mrs. Duffy, I didn't mean to have at you. It's just that . . . I *am* sure. I love Edward; I'd not be happy with anyone else."

"Oh, my dear girl. Love is a curious thing." Mrs. Duffy's eyes softened. "And it doesn't let us rest easy, eh?"

* * *

Mr. O'Leary talked to Paddy about moving west. "You're welcome, lad, to come with us," he said.

"I couldn't do that," the boy replied. "Mr. Dooley needs me. So does Whacker." He grinned and puffed up his chest. "I sat next to the mayor himself at the Sons of Ireland breakfast this morning. I'm going to be a big swell one of these days; you'll see."

"And so he might," said Mr. O'Leary, recounting the story to Maureen. "There's no denying he has a way about him. He's good brains in his head, as well."

Maureen rolled her eyes. "Mule brains if you ask me. Stubborn."

That night Maureen went up on the roof of the lodging house to be by herself. It was quiet there; she could sort out her thoughts in peace. What was she to do? Edward and the O'Learys would be leaving soon; Brian had found a happy life in Boston. Da was working for a blacksmith in Canada and might move west himself, in time. She thought about the Cabots' cellar with its endless piles of laundry, and about Mr. Mellen's earnest smile when she received a perfect mark in her speller.

Somewhere a woman began to sing a lullaby; her song drifted up and across the rooftops, stirring Maureen's loneliness. From the garden behind St. Brendan's Church came the smell of early lilac and Maureen was reminded of the wild bushes that grew along the hedgerows in Ireland.

Ireland? Had she really once lived in such a place? There had been a mother and a father then, a sister, two brothers. There had been a cottage, with the Cooley Hills slumbering nearby. Aye, a long time ago such things had been her life, but now they were gone.

27
Good-by to New York

The room on Oliver Street looked abandoned. The kettle was gone, the woodbox empty, the cupboards bare. In the corner were several burlap bags, filled and made fast for the long journey ahead.

Because of the late spring, Mr. O'Leary and Edward had decided to take the overland route to St. Louis and avoid risking a flatboat on the flood-swollen Ohio. Their plans called for crossing to Jersey and taking the train as far as Hagerstown, where wagon masters organized traveling parties heading west. They would join with one there and go on to St. Louis.

Maureen was finishing her packing. She took down the crucifix and holy water vial, remembering the morning Ma had given them to her. One day she would find a snug cottage in which to hang them again. Somewhere in Missouri, perhaps.

She packed the crucifix and vial away. Everything was ready for the departure the next morning. She had said her farewells to Miss Trump and the others at the Cabots', and also to the Rothmans. That left only Paddy, for Mrs. Duffy would be coming down to the ferry to say good-by.

172

As she was heading for the door, Maureen stopped and thought about the crucifix. It had been given to Ma by Granny. And Ma had given it to her, to bring to America. All at once she returned to her satchel and removed the small wooden cross. She put it in her pocket and went out the door.

Paddy and two other boys were lounging in front of Dooley's headquarters. "Funny," said Maureen to herself. "Da's cap seems almost to fit Paddy now. Is it my imagination or has he grown taller?"

The boys saw her coming. His two companions nudged Paddy and went off, leaving him alone.

"Hello, Paddy."

"Hello."

"I . . . came to say good-by. We're leaving in the morning, you know."

He squinted and looked back over his shoulder to where his friends waited.

"If you've changed your mind . . . you can still come with us."

"That's O.K. I'm staying."

For a moment they stood looking at each other.

"Paddy, I'll write to you if you want. Could I send the letters here?" She nodded up at the building.

"I guess."

"We're taking the early ferry to Jersey, to get the train." Maureen forced a smile. "You could come down to the docks and wave us off."

"I dunno," he said, hunching his shoulders. "Looks like it might rain tomorrow."

"Well, then I guess I'd better say good-by now." Her hand went to the crucifix in her pocket. She held it out to him. "I'd like you to have this. Remember? It was Ma's, from Granny."

173

He took the crucifix and turned it over, looking at it, keeping his head down. "Thanks, Maureen," he mumbled, then turned and ran up the street past his waiting companions.

The O'Leary children needed a good prodding to get them up and on their way to the ferry slip. Edward had arrived at half-five to help Mr. O'Leary load bags and satchels onto the trundle cart. His own possessions, including his carpenter's tools, were rolled into the sailcloth duffle bag which he slung across his back.

Mrs. Duffy had anticipated the children's crankiness and presented each of them with a freshly baked cinnamon bun. The food made the long trek to the pier easier.

"I'm going to miss you," Maureen said to Mrs. Duffy as the two of them walked together behind the trundle cart. "I don't know what any of us would have done without your help."

"Oh, you'd have managed somehow. People do."

"I'll write to you as soon as I'm able, Mrs. Duffy."

"I know you will." Mrs. Duffy lowered her voice. "There is one thing I wanted to mention, Maureen. Perhaps it hasn't come up yet, in all the talk about St. Louis."

"Oh, what's that?"

"Missouri is a slave state. Some people there will be slave-holders."

"You mean the same as down south?"

"That's right. But it's also a border state, meaning there's free states right next door. Letty Trump says many runaways come through Missouri. St. Louis is within shouting distance of free Illinois.

"I'm telling you this because a day might come when you're asked to help, like before."

174

"But to live where there are slaves, I'll not like that, Mrs. Duffy."

"Exactly. And there will be others like you, feeling the same. Your voices need to be heard. You can help end slavery by speaking out against it."

"But one person can't—"

"One person on every street, in every town and city, that's many voices. You'll see."

They were nearing the Weehawken ferry slip. Dozens of people were already lined up, waiting to board.

Mr. O'Leary looked around. "Just as well we're early. I hadn't expected such a crowd."

"Get in line, Maureen," said Mrs. Duffy. "No tears, now. Good luck to you, and God bless."

Maureen put her arms around Mrs. Duffy. "Good-by. Thank you for everything." Her eyes filled with tears despite the woman's order. "You'll watch out for Paddy?"

"Of course."

The O'Learys and Edward said their good-bys to Mrs. Duffy. "Hurry now," she said, pushing them toward the gangplank. "Get a place at the railing for the children."

Maureen took Jenny O'Leary into her arms lest the little girl be lost in the milling crowd. Jenny put her fingers against Maureen's wet cheeks.

"Why crying, Maureen? Hurt?"

"No, Jenny. Only sad, is all." Maureen saw Edward looking at her. "And happy, too."

They went up the gangplank onto the ferry. Everyone jostled for a place at the railing and began waving to the well-wishers below.

Maureen scanned the dock and quayside, hoping Paddy had come to say good-by after all. There was no sign of him. People waved handkerchiefs and hats, making a colorful flutter that pleased Jenny.

The ferry gave a lurch and Maureen grabbed hold of the railing, steadying herself. Edward came alongside her. "Come here, bunny rabbit," he said to Jenny. "I'll hold you." He took the little girl and gave her his kerchief to wave at Mrs. Duffy.

"Maureen," he said, "do you see who's down there, near the moorings?"

She leaned forward, looking in the direction he pointed.

"Off to the left, wearing the brown cap."

Paddy O'Connor was shinning his way up one of the pier timbers. When he reached the top, his eyes went to the row of faces along the ferry railing.

"Paddy! Paddy! Over here!" Maureen shouted and waved her arms.

He saw her. For a moment he only stared, watching the ferry slowly edge away from the dock. Then he took off Da's cap and waved it at her, back and forth.

"Good-by, Paddy! God bless!" Maureen called. She could not hear if he replied.

She clung to the railing, waving until the boy and the cap had blurred into the long curve of the New York harbor.

"We'll meet again, one day," she said softly. "All of us."

For a long time she gazed down at the water. When at last she turned and faced westward, the Jersey shore loomed near at hand. She smiled at Edward. Already there was a change in the air.